The bird had been gliding a quarter mile or more out from the blind and several hundreds of feet up in the air, but now it tightened its circle and began to bank downward and closer to the blind. Sam had been tracking and filming it for several minutes. While he prepared to use the zoom lens on the bird's closing flight, Sam realized suddenly that as focused as he had been on the big eagle, Lucy had never really left his mind. He had been thinking of Lucy as he had felt, sensed, the bird's first stirrings; and he was thinking of her now as he rotated the lens, drawing the bird rapidly into closer focus. Sam refocused on the white head and zoomed again, pulling the image rapidly into close resolution. There was the crown of white feathers and then the golden flashing disk—the eye fierce and intelligent. Sam backed off slightly now with the zoom and within the frame, like some ghostly double exposure emerging from the strange refractions of the Quabbin woods, another image hovered—the face of Lucy Swift.

"No!" he whispered. But the double image remained.

KATHRYN LASKY has written several novels for young people, including *Beyond the Divide* and *Prank*, both named ALA Best Books for Young Adults and both available in Dell Laurel-Leaf editions. Ms. Lasky lives with her husband and two children in Cambridge, Massachusetts.

ALSO AVAILABLE IN LAUREL-LEAF BOOKS:

QUANTITY SALES

Most Dell Books are available at special quantity discounts when purchased in bulk by corporations, organizations, and special-interest groups. Custom imprinting or excerpting can also be done to fit special needs. For details write: Dell Publishing Co., Inc., 666 Fifth Avenue, New York, NY 10103. Attn.: Special Sales Dept.

INDIVIDUAL SALES

Are there any Dell Books you want but cannot find in your local stores? If so, you can order them directly from us. You can get any Dell book in print. Simply include the book's title, author, and ISBN number, if you have it, along with a check or money order (no cash can be accepted) for the full retail price plus $1.50 to cover shipping and handling. Mail to: Dell Readers Service, P.O. Box 5057, Des Plaines, IL 60017.

HOME FREE
KATHRYN LASKY

LAUREL-LEAF BOOKS

LAUREL-LEAF BOOKS bring together under a single imprint outstanding works of fiction and nonfiction particularly suitable for young adult readers, both in and out of the classroom. Charles F. Reasoner, Professor Emeritus of Children's Literature and Reading, New York University, is consultant to this series.

Published by
Dell Publishing Co., Inc.
1 Dag Hammarskjold Plaza
New York, New York 10017

Laurel-Leaf Library ® TM 766734, Dell Publishing Co., Inc.

ISBN: 0-440-20038-5

RL: 6.3

Reprinted by arrangement with Macmillan Publishing Company

Printed in the United States of America

January 1988

10 9 8 7 6 5 4 3 2 1

WFH

1 AN ACCIDENTAL WILDERNESS

ONE

There were babies all over the place—crawling up the legs of furniture and parents, crying, sucking bottles, screaming "more," "mine" and "no," the three words that seemed, to Sam Brooks, to constitute the totality of baby ethics. How come there were so many babies on his mom's side of the family? There wasn't one kid his age at this family gathering.

"Here, have some of this sourdough bread with your dinner," his Aunt Marie said, coming up to him with a basket. "I do wish Jamie were here for you, Sam, but he and his school pals went off on a cross-country-ski trip with their history teacher from the academy. Julia is the only other cousin near your age, and she's in France with the Experiment in International Living."

Sam wondered if any kids in the East went to schools

with normal names like Kokomo High and experimented with living at home.

"It must be a terrible bore for you, sweetie," Marie continued.

"Oh, no, no," he lied. It wasn't just that it was a bore. It was too hot in his Aunt Peggy and Uncle Marlon's house. There were too many people. The antique early-American furniture was too spindly, the cushions too thin. And, finally, he was just sick of being their pet orphan, or half-orphan, he guessed it was, since only one of his parents was gone.

It seemed as if every five minutes some robust uncle or male cousin of his mom's would come up to him, clap him on the back, call him "pal" or, worse, "son," and say, "How ya doing? Like fishing? Skiing? Sailing?" Sam had never skied or sailed in his life, and when he fished he liked to do it alone. Didn't anybody ever bowl here? Play miniature golf? Sam looked around the crowded room. If Sears Roebuck had a catalogue of father figures, he thought, there was one of each model here tonight—and none too subtle. *Your basic Father Figure/Dad comes in cord or wool-plaid, water-repellent shirt. Slightly balding, bald, or thick gray curls. Mustache optional. Solid shoulder slaps, industrial strength or regular.*

A man in a red-plaid shirt, quite bald, with bright pink cheeks and wire-rim glasses, was making his way toward Sam.

"Hi, son!"

"Hello, Uncle Albert," Sam said rather pointedly.

"You know, I got a little hunting cabin up in the White Mountains. You ever gone hunting?"

"No—well, actually, I used to shoot rats out in Indiana

on my grandfather's farm. They'd get into the chicken house."

"Oh, no! no! This isn't the same thing at all. No, you ever been in the middle of a stand of birch trees in the crisp dawn of an October morning in New England with a doe in your sights? Dropped one last season. One swift shot right in her heart. She dropped right there. A good clean kill." His eyes narrowed as he reenvisioned the scene. "Just as those first flares of sun spread up over the horizon . . ." His voice tapered off.

Sam nibbled at his bread. "Mine weren't so clean."

"What's that?" Uncle Albert asked, suddenly coming back from the stand of birches in the crisp dawn of a New England October.

"The rats. It was a real mess. Especially when I used the .22 with hollow points. Rat guts splattered all over the place. Gram got so mad she went and bought me an air rifle." Uncle Albert's rather small mouth twitched slightly. His eyes grew dull behind his glasses.

"Well, yes. I should think so!"

"Yeah, Gram said it was enough to make the chickens quit laying. But then she got me the air rifle and I just picked them off nice and neat."

"*Rats?*" Uncle Albert was staring at him, hard.

"Night. That's the best time to get them." Sam couldn't seem to stop himself. Uncle Albert was looking desperately around for his wife, Nez. "Quite a challenge, actually, trying to shoot a black rat at night in a dark chicken house."

"Yes! Yes! Warm in here, isn't it?" Uncle Albert mopped his brow and twisted his neck around. "Oh, there's Nez!" he exclaimed joyously. "Well, it's not the same thing at all as deer hunting, young man." He had started to turn away from Sam and was giving him a few pats on the shoulder—weak, non-industrial-strength ones.

"Well, it's all killing, I guess," Sam said almost gaily. The plump hand stopped, midpat. Albert excused himself and hurried over to his wife's side. She was fussing with a dish of something at the buffet.

"The boy needs help, Nez!" he said, not quite out of earshot.

"I need help!" Nez was sticking some parsley into a gaping wound in a red gelatin ring. "I make this aspic fifteen times a year and why does it decide not to unmold tonight? Harry!" She called to a tall, thin man a few feet from her with his back to the buffet. "You're a plastic surgeon. What would you do in this situation?"

Harry turned around and looked at the aspic. "Eat it!"

"The boy is seriously disturbed," Albert whispered hoarsely.

"The boy!" said Nez. "Sam has lost his father and moved halfway across the country. You'd be disturbed too."

"You know what he just said to me about hunting?"

"What?" Nez spooned lasagna onto her plate.

"I'd just finished telling him about the doe I got last season and he starts to tell me about shooting rats in his grandfather's chicken house out in Indiana with hollow-point bullets and . . ."

"It's all killing, Albert."

"Oh, Lord!"

"QUORP's plan is for the birds, Marlon." The three men, two uncles and his mother's cousin Leo, were standing a few feet away from Sam. Overhearing some of Uncle

Albert's conversation with Aunt Nez, he had retired to a cushion in the corner of the room.

"It will never pass," said Leo emphatically.

"That's good," said the other uncle. "Although I don't really see that opening up the northeast corner would be all that bad. It might appease them some."

"They'd just want more," Marlon answered quickly. "We lost the valley once. Let's not lose this too."

"Is Gus Early well enough to be back in the fray?"

"Leo would know more about that." Both men turned attentively to the man next to them.

"Listen, sick as he's been, that guy has never been out of the fray. He's totally committed to those birds."

What birds, Sam wondered. He was trying to listen, but a baby had just rounded a nearby armchair and was launching an attack. Its tiny fists were burrowing into Sam's lasagna.

"No, baby. No, no. Here, you want to learn how to eat nice?" Sam lifted a fork with a small amount of lasagna on it. The baby opened its mouth and ate it. "Good baby. Want more?"

"Rrrrh, mo!"

"Okay, here's another bite. What's your name, baby?"

"Mo."

"More—that's your name? Okay, More. Many famous Mores—Thomas More. I did a term paper on him for my Western Civ class. Marianne Moore—she's a poet. One of her poems was in my anthology for English. Clement Moore—he wrote ' 'Twas the Night Before Christmas.' I'm sure you know that."

"The eagle reintroduction program is going to do more for Gus Early than any chemotherapy, believe me."

Sam swung his attention from the baby to the three

men. "This would interest you, Sam," Leo said, noticing his gaze.

"My dad did a lot of research on eagles. You know, DDT and its effect of eggshell thinning. That kind of stuff."

"He would have been very interested in the Quabbin Reservoir, then. No DDT has ever been used there. No pesticides at all. The eagles have a good chance of making it there. This fellow Early came up with the idea of bringing young eaglets in, with hopes of establishing them as nesting birds."

Sam had disengaged himself from the baby and walked over to the three men. "How come pesticides have never been used there?"

"Well, the Quabbin is the water supply for all of Boston," Leo said, "And before that . . ." He paused.

"What was it before?" Sam asked.

"It's a long story, but before it was a reservoir it was a valley with four towns—Enfield, Greenwich, Prescott and Dana. That was before DDT."

"What happened to the towns? The valley?"

"Flooded. Drowned," Leo said quickly.

"What's happening over there to your dinner, Sam?" Marlon asked. They all turned toward the corner where Sam had been sitting. The baby was shoving double-fisted loads of lasagna into his mouth.

"Oh, no!" Sam rushed over to rescue his plate and the Oriental rug. "Well, at least it blends in," he muttered as he tried to wipe up the mess with his napkin.

The baby by this time had eaten half of Sam's lasagna. "Maybe, More, you should think about changing your name to Less. You know, you're kind of tubby. What's becoming in a baby does not wear well in years to come. Try those folds of fat and zits on your face at the same time. You'll be a real loser then." He had better shut up. He saw his mother's sister-in-law, the baby's mother, coming toward them.

"Hi, Sam. You and Jessie getting on?" She was real pretty, Roberta. Her voice was just a little too sweet. "You ever do baby-sitting?"

"Well, I have, but right now I'm just concentrating on getting settled here."

"Of course," said Roberta. "It's quite an adjustment, I'm sure."

"Yeah." The understatement of the year, Sam thought. He looked across the room. His mother sat next to her father, a curved wraith of a man in a wheelchair. He had a fringe of fine white hair that swirled around the edges of his bald scalp like mare's-tail clouds on a windy day. Philippa Brooks's head was bent close to her father's mouth so she could listen to the weak, raspy voice. She was smiling under her mass of auburn curls, Sam could tell. He could imagine her eyes in crinkled merriment. He could see her mouth clearly, though. He could read the word her lips had just formed. *Home.*

How could it be home for her and not for him?

TWO

"I think Gus Early would be more than happy to take you out to the Quabbin to do some eagle watching," Leo said as he turned out of the driveway to take Sam and his mother home after the party. "Would you be interested?"

"Sure."

"What's this?" Philippa asked.

"Gus Early," Leo said. "You might not remember him. He's an old Enfielder and a friend of your dad's. He's been pretty sick lately."

"Oh, is he the eagle man Dad was talking about?"

"That's the one."

"Well, he certainly can't be strong enough to hike in there with Sam."

"Oh, he's tough, and this reintroduction project is

virtually his lifeline. He's bound and determined to get to Manitoba this summer."

"What's in Manitoba?" Philippa asked.

"Young eagles. They'll be newly hatched in June."

"What does he want with them?"

"Well, he flies up there with some people from the National Wildlife Federation. There are literally millions of acres of wilderness—lakes, woods—great eagle country. They fly over in float planes, spot the nests. When they spot one with two eaglets, they land. The climbers go up and take one."

"Must be kind of sad for the parents," Sam said.

"Yes," echoed his mother.

"But," Leo said, "they always leave one baby. They have to do it at just the right time—when the eaglets know that they are eagles but haven't learned what their home territory is."

"You mean they haven't imprinted yet?" Sam asked.

"That's right. And they can't fly yet either."

"Then what happens?" Philippa asked.

"They put them in travel cages and bring them back here," Leo continued. "Gus has built a hacking tower down by the edge of the Quabbin."

"A hacking tower?" Sam and Philippa asked at the same time.

"Sort of a man-made foster nest for young birds to be reared in for a few weeks. Gus and his helpers drop food into the cages through an opening and observe them through one-way glass. When they think the eagles are old enough to fly, they release them."

"And then?" said Philippa.

"They hope."

"Hope what?" she asked.

"Hope that the eagles have come to think of the Quabbin as home and will return to breed. It's safe here," Leo replied.

"From what? People?" Philippa asked.

"And pesticides. As I was saying earlier, they never sprayed the Quabbin," Leo said. "Here we are, folks." He turned into the driveway of Sam and his mother's new house.

"That's all very intriguing," Philippa said as she unlocked the door. "It's nice to think of a place," she yawned, "that's never been sprayed with DDT, isn't it?"

"Yeah, I guess so," Sam said.

"You guess?" Philippa's tone was slightly perplexed.

"I was just wondering what happened to the towns like Enfield. Seems like a lot of people around here were 'old Enfielders' or 'old Prescotters' or 'old Dana folks.' They didn't spray, but a lot of people sure were moved out."

"I don't know that much about it, really," Philippa said, turning on the kitchen lights. "Want anything to eat?"

"Naw."

"Drink?"

"I'll take some milk."

"Me too," she said, going to the refrigerator.

"How come you don't know anything about it, Mom?"

"About what?"

"Enfield, Dana, Prescott, the other one . . ."

"Greenwich."

"Yeah. How come? You come from here. Your whole family comes from here."

"Here!" Philippa said with emphasis. "New Salem, Orange, Petersham, Pelham—but not Enfield or Dana or Prescott or Greenwich. Besides, it all happened before I was born. You want your milk hot?"

"No. Yuck!"

She handed him a glass and poured her own into a saucepan. "It's better than sleeping pills." Philippa rubbed her eyes and sat on a stool next to the stove.

"I wonder what it was like back then."

"What? When?" Philippa asked absently.

"Those towns—underwater."

"They're not underwater. They tore them down first."

"What about the people? Where'd they go?"

"I don't know. Still a lot around, like Gus Early. Dad would have liked the notion of this project, wouldn't he?" Philippa spoke softly and stared out the kitchen window that hung like a black square on the winter night.

"You mean the reintroduction thing for eagles?"

"Yes." She paused. "Remember when Dad took the . . ." Sam remembered before she had finished the sentence. He knew what she was going to say. It was the photograph that Philippa was about to refer to. It had become known as "that picture." The image itself was too horrifying to talk about. It was a photograph taken by David Brooks some years before on a summer research trip to a place in Michigan known to have a breeding population of eagles.

It was a photograph of an eaglet embryo. The embryo looked perfect except for one fact: it was held only within the inner membrane, the transparent sac. There was no shell, no protection. It would never hatch. It might as well have died within the first trillionth of a second of being laid. The chemical contaminants that had been sprayed in the air had traveled through the food chain and accumulated to unprecedented levels in the parent eagles until the shells they laid were not ten or twenty-five percent thinner, but simply gone.

Philippa Brooks, although disinclined toward science and by her own admission no nature freak, had been deeply disturbed by the picture. The image had come back again and again to haunt her. They had never really spoken much about the picture, but now Philippa rubbed her finger around the rim of the cup until it made a high, nervous little squeak in the silence of the winter night.

"You know," she began hesitantly. Her face was flushed a bit, and Sam saw the two familiar spots of color that often appeared on her temples where her auburn hair swept back. "Well." She hesitated again. "You know that picture? I just"—she ran her fingers through her hair and spoke rapidly—"can't seem to forget that image of that embryo in its transparent sac, that membrane. It's so weird. At first I found it just repulsive—sickening. But once I . . ." Sam was looking intently at Philippa. "I think once I got beyond the physical revulsion, well, the image has just kept returning. It's as if it were a baby orphaned before it was born."

Sam took a swallow of milk and looked at his mom. Sometimes, he just didn't know what to say. It seemed all wrong that he was the only one here with his mother. The ratio was even, but unfair—one kid, one adult. "Maybe we should go to sleep, Mom." That was all he could come up with in the way of comfort.

The bedrooms were on the east side of the house. They had large windows to catch the morning sun, and at night the newly installed skylights allowed Sam in his room and Philippa in hers to follow the moon's and the stars' tracery across the sky. Tonight, however, when they went to bed, the skylights framed racing clouds that smoked the March night. There was not a star's dim pulse or even a tarnished streak of moonlight.

Several hours later, as they slept and the rising moon gained a purchase on the dome of night, Sam and his mother dreamed. It was the same dream, but each one dreamed it slightly differently, so that their individual images blended like the separate but concordant tones of a chord. The dream was of things alone but not free—wingless wanderers and numbed orphans. It was the dream of the shell-less eaglet embryo.

A thin blade of moonlight crossed her face. Philippa was instantly awake. The sky had cleared and the moon swam directly above her. She wondered briefly if it was the moon or the dream that had startled her. She knew she would not be able to sleep again that night. She got up and wrapped herself in an old plaid robe and slipped her feet into her fleece-lined bedroom slippers.

In the bedroom across the hall Sam heard her and woke up. Often his mother could not sleep. It never seemed to bother her. She always found plenty to do at these odd hours. One May night at their old house he had looked out his window to see his mother quietly planting a border of petunias along the front walk. He turned over and sank back into a dreamless sleep.

Philippa went downstairs to a room, a blank, unpainted room with no floor covering except plywood. The old boards, warped and dull, had been taken out for refinishing. An English desk of dark walnut with a myriad of cubbyholes faced a newly built bay window. In one corner was an old but very elegant sewing machine that operated with a foot treadle. Someday the room would be a snug study and sewing room and the window would look out on a Japanese garden that Philippa was planning. She took a notebook from the central drawer of her desk and began writing. Two hours later she finished.

Shell-less

To be unborn and yet an orphan,
To lie scalded by too bright a moon
And sliced by slants of sunlight.
To never know the soft oblivion of sleep before birth,
Of liquid rhythms in the shielding curves.
To be shell-less and in terror,
To be taunted by the flicker of life
Then consumed by the blaze.
The mother peers uncomprehending at the trans-
    lucent sac.
The beak is just forming.
The eye, large within, stares out.

THREE

By the time Sam came down for breakfast the next morning, his mother had already scraped the paint from ten feet of molding in the dining room. Her hair was tied up in a kerchief, and pale green flecks of paint were scattered across her face. Sam had been hearing her scrape away since he had first wakened half an hour before and had purposely stayed in bed to avoid having to join in the restoration activities. People didn't fix up houses around here, he thought. They restored them, and his mom seemed to be restoring theirs with an energy and enthusiasm that made him feel weak, just to watch.

He had to admit that this was the happiest he had seen her since his dad's death. "A focus—you have a focus now, Philippa." That's what Aunt Nez had said. Her job teaching high-school English had not provided that for the past year. Of her own admission she had sleepwalked her way through teaching Shakespeare— "And when you start getting bored with *Macbeth* it's time to quit," she had said.

Sam stood now in his pajamas and blinked sleepily at the figure on the ladder. "Were you really bored with *Macbeth*, Mom?"

Philippa stopped scraping, looked down at her son, smiled and scratched her head. "No, not really." And before he could ask, she said, "So now you're wondering why I'm scraping paint. A more monotonous job there is not, right?"

"Well, yes, right."

"I wasn't bored with *Macbeth*, Sam. I was bored with teaching—teaching *Macbeth* year in, year out. It's nice to be able to read something and know you're not going to have to explain it, come up with anything profound. I just didn't want to do that anymore, not to mention that the prospect of teaching *As You Like It* to the likes of Hogg Wilmot and Chugg Larrabee was less than inspiring."

Sam laughed at this. "But don't worry," she said climbing down the ladder. "You don't have to scrape paint."

"Oh, I will," Sam offered. "I don't mind."

"Come off it, Sam. Don't kill me with your enthusiasm." She ran her fingers through his hair.

"No, I'll scrape!" he said, trying to pump some eagerness into his voice.

"Look, Sam," she said, taking him by the shoulders and facing him squarely. "You don't have to want to do this, and don't feel bad about it. I do not expect fifteen-year-old kids to be interested in restoring eighteenth-century New England farmhouses. My restoration is not necessarily yours. Different strokes for different folks, as they say. You've got some free time now before school starts. Have some fun."

"You mean read *As You Like It*?" Sam laughed.

"For Pete's sake, no! Go out and explore. You've hardly seen New Salem."

"It's only two blocks long."

"Well, there's North New Salem. It's almost two blocks long."

"What's in North New Salem?"

"A couple of houses and the Swift River Valley Historical Society."

"What's that?"

"Just a historical society. A lot about the towns that were here before the reservoir. You had a lot of questions about that. You could go and find some answers, maybe."

But there seemed to be only more questions.

"I'm going home for a sandwich, Sam." The elderly lady poked her head in the door of the Enfield Room where Sam had been reading old newspapers for the past two hours.

"It's lunchtime?" Sam looked up, startled.

"Past, I'd say." The woman smiled. "Twelve forty-five. You didn't hear my stomach growling?"

"Oh, gee, I'm sorry."

"No! No trouble. You stay on. I'll be back in half an hour. I've got the Eastham Button Club coming in at two. No rush."

Sam heard her descend the uncarpeted wooden staircase. He had no idea that he had been here that long. Time seemed indeed to have stopped, which he supposed was sort of the purpose of a historical society. But why should time stop for him? Why should this interest him, Sam Brooks, Kokomo, Indiana, Hoosier transplant? He had no connection here. Well, his mother did come from New England; but he was a Midwesterner. He didn't even like New England. It was too close, too cozy. Towns here were too near one another, roads too narrow, and horizons too cluttered with trees and hills. But nonetheless, here he was, reading an account of the past, a valley's past, of four towns that were no more, that were intentionally wiped off the map almost fifty years before.

He had stopped counting, but the 1938 issues of the *Springfield Republican Union* reported at least fifty-three farewell parties, not for people, but for organizations and towns. A framed poster on the wall of the room in which he sat announced the farewell ball of the Enfield Fire Department—Wednesday, April 27, 1938, eight to twelve, "A Last Good Time for All." He had read about the last meeting of the Quabbin Valley Ladies' Club, as well as the last mail posted from the Dana post office. There was a picture of the postmistress with a weak smile and a bunch of letters in her hand. The last run of the Rabbit, the train that went through the valley, had been reported, and oddest of all was the story he had been reading when Mrs. Clark poked her head in to say she was going to lunch. It was a newspaper report of Enfield's last town meeting during which "propertyless citizens" met and voted eighteen hundred dollars to buy a monument. On one side the monument would memorialize World War I veterans and on the other—"since no Enfield men had died in the Spanish American War"—it would memorialize the living townspeople of Enfield—themselves.

"Weird," he whispered. He read another paragraph. "Really weird." His eyes opened wider. "Since by this time next year there will be no Enfield, as the town shall be under water, the monument is to be erected in the Quabbin Park Cemetery, where exhumed bodies from the cemeteries of Enfield and the other three towns have been reburied."

Sam's stomach grumbled only once in the next hour while he read a sentimental account of a Boston lady's reminiscence of the valley, in which she referred to "captivating little towns" and how the view from the old Greenwich Country Club had been beautiful to the point of distracting her from her tennis and, indeed, her serve was off. Also sentimental, but a lot more palatable and possessing the sledgehammer cadences of Henry Wadsworth Longfellow, was a poem written by a certain Samuel Ritchie of Enfield and recited by his daughter Persis at a graduation ceremony in Belchertown. Sam copied down the last stanza to show his mother—"Once an English-teacher's son, always!" he muttered as he wrote down the lines.

> So old Enfield is demolished
> Gone are spots which once we cherished.
> Gone forever, yea forever
> Are the Red Man's hunting grounds.
> Let us climb again up Quabbin
> Just once more before the parting.
> There is water in the valley
> And the silv'ry river's gone.
> Gone are churches, farms, and dwellings
> Gone are trees and fertile meadows.
> Nothing left but just the water
> Where the Red Man's feet once trod.
> So the moral of this story
> All man's deeds will not bring glory.
> Let our lives be for each other

Let us yet love one another
From this day and evermore.

"So the moral of this story / All man's deeds will not bring glory." Isn't that the truth, Sam thought as he trudged through the soupy remnants of an old snowfall. He crossed Route 202, which seemed more like a country lane than a highway, and continued toward his home. On the other side of 202 was a small road. The asphalt petered out to gravel within twenty feet, and a chain-link fence with a gate stretched across it. In the middle of the gate was a sign that read DEAD END ST MDC GATE 25. Gates twenty-eight and twenty-nine were at the end of the street where Sam lived, a quarter mile from his house. These gates, belonging to the Massachusetts Department of Conservation, led into the Quabbin Reservoir.

What kind of a nutso place had he moved to, Sam thought. Exhumed bodies, war memorials doubling as monuments to living townspeople, and dead-end gates on every street. God almighty, why couldn't he be back in Indiana—on the experiment in farm living with Gram and Grandpa? How many days was it till haying—ninety-four, more or less?

Well, if it was a good dry spring, maybe eighty-seven.

Sam burst into the kitchen. His mother was working on the molding in there now. Standing at attention, he recited:

"So old Kokomo is abolished
Gone the cornfields and the Chryslers
And the drive-in movies dimmed

And old Hogg with voice so grim
As he recites man's seven stages
And lets the piglets out of cages."

"Sam?" Philippa giggled softly, but somewhat nervously. "You all right?"

FOUR

"They call it an accident." The older man turned to Sam and gestured with his head toward the small opening of the blind. "An accidental wilderness." He spoke in a night-hushed voice.

"An accidental wilderness?" Sam whispered. It seemed like an odd reversal of things—to call something wild an accident. He shifted his body slightly so he could see the man better. They were both crouched on pallets in the ingenious structure, a blind for wildlife observation that had been designed to look like a beaver lodge. Inside, in addition to the two pallets, there was a small gas burner for heat and cooking. A coffee pot gurgled on it now. Against the southeast side of the blind was a platform. On it was mounted a 16mm Bolex camera with a 300mm lens poised at one of three small openings in the wall. There was a second camera positioned nearby. Now it was dark outside, however, and the lens stared into a night sky that was pricked with the light of thousands of stars.

"Yeah." The man laughed softly. "That's how it is now—nature is an accident."

"Seems funny."

"It is funny. It really wasn't planned to happen this way. It was the only good thing that came out of flooding the valley." He was quiet for a moment. "How long you been here now, Sam?" he asked.

"Two weeks."

"Thought you'd been here longer than that."

"Nope. Just two weeks, ten hours and"—Sam looked at his watch—"twenty-two minutes."

"You keep track of things," the old man said.

"Not much else to do."

"School still on March break?"

"Yeah."

"Guess your mom thought this would be a good time to move, with the break here and all. Give you a chance to settle in."

"Good time"—the words rippled meaninglessly in Sam's brain. It really wasn't a good time or an appropriate time or any special time. It was just time, according to his mother. They had tried it alone for fifteen months. That was how long it had been since his father had died in the crash on Route 465. They were doing okay. At least Sam had thought so. Life went on. Not as normal; nothing would ever be normal after that call that split the night, changing everything forever. But in general they were "functioning"—a favorite word Sam's grandfather used when he would call up three or four times a week from the East. Functioning with the help of friends, and a therapist for his mom. Sam had refused to go after one session. "I don't know what time she thought it was," Sam said suddenly, turning to the old man.

Gus Early looked up at the boy. Sam's face was thin and sharply angled, with high cheekbones under ruddy cheeks flushed with bronze freckles. A thatch of blue-black hair fell down on his narrow forehead, framing his gray eyes. The eyes appeared impassive, almost calm. But looking harder Gus Early saw something else—a flicker. He had seen it before in animals' eyes, deer late in February, winter-hungry and scared.

"She just decided to move," Gus said. It was not a question.

"Yeah." Sam paused. "She just got up one morning, looked out the window and said, 'I'm sick of flat.' "

"Flat?" Gus said.

"Yeah." Sam's eyes crinkled and a smile began. A thin silver wire stretched across his front teeth.

"You come from Flat, Indiana, or something?"

"No. Kokomo. She meant flatness. That's what she said, at least. 'I'm sick of flatness and cornfields and shopping malls and Chryslers.' "

"Chryslers?"

"Yeah. There's a big Chrysler plant in Kokomo. That's where most people worked, except for my Dad."

"What did he do?"

"Taught high-school biology."

"That's right." Gus shook his head in a gesture of sudden memory. "That's what your Grandpa Eastman told me. So your mom got sick of it all. She just wanted to come back here to where her folks live. You get sick of flat too?"

"Naw. Not really. When it's flat you can always imagine mountains; and I liked the fields. My grandpa out there, my dad's dad, he has a farm. Two years ago he bought himself a brand-new New Holland stack loader for haying. Thirty thousand dollars, air-conditioned cab and tape deck too! Guess what?" Sam's eyes were bright now. The scared look was gone.

"What?"

"He said if I read the entire manual and tested out, I could operate it." He paused. "Guess who's been doing his haying for the last two years?"

"You?"

"Me! Since I was thirteen," Sam said, his eyes glowing now. "Mom promised me I can go back this summer for haying. It's the greatest feeling in the world being up there eight feet above the ground, good music in your ears—and those fields. You look across to a field of uncut hay. You know what it looks like when the wind moves through it?"

"What?"

"Water—a river or a whole darned ocean!"

"See any eagles?" Gus asked.

"No. Never saw one in my life—that's why I'm here." It suddenly struck Sam as slightly peculiar that he was sitting in this blind with this old man, Gus Early, who was chief photographer of the State Division of Fisheries and Wildlife. Eagles were Gus's main interest, and now, for these brief hours, it was Sam's purpose to see an eagle. For the past fifteen months it had seemed as if Sam's life had been filled with tasks but no purpose.

In the dim light of the blind Sam studied Gus's profile. The face scored with lines, the cheeks sunken, the jaw sharply squared—these belonged to an old man. But not the eye. Fierce and intelligent, wild yet knowing, it shone with the intensity of an eagle's.

"Mr. Early."

The old head snapped around. "Call me Gus."

"Gus." Sam paused. "When you were talking before about its being an accident, an accidental wilderness, where exactly is 'it'?"

The old man was looking out the opening where the lens faced, but even from the side Sam could see the light in his eye grow softer, as if a veil had dropped. Then he swung full face toward Sam.

"Out there." Gus cranked the lens so it protruded through the opening. "Here, take a look. Dawn light is up. You'll be able to catch a glimpse."

Sam crawled over to the platform where the camera rested and put his eye against the eyepiece. Through the bare branches of the trees he saw a blur in the early-morning light, a smear of gray against which the trees looked like black embroidery. "Here, let me focus for you," Gus said, and began turning a knob. The trees began to soften. "Tell me when it's sharp," he said. The smear slowly grew clearer.

"Sharp!" Sam said, and inhaled suddenly. Now he could see it. He could see the ripples, a curl of foam near the shore, an island rising a mile or so offshore and then, beyond, more water and no shore. It was the largest body of water he had ever seen except for the Atlantic Ocean. Was it an ocean? No, a valley, Gus had said.

He turned his eye away from the camera. "It's hard to believe it was a valley."

"Was, is—it's hard to know how to talk about it." Gus laughed. "Now it's the Quabbin Reservoir. Four hundred and twelve billion gallons of water fill that valley."

"Four hundred and twelve billion gallons! That's an unimaginable number."

"I know."

The water was shimmering now with the first strokes of the day's sun. Silver glints fingered out over the surface, turning the water platinum and smooth. In another few minutes, when the sun was higher, the ripples reappeared and the water moved with a rosy darkness. Sam pressed against the rubber cup of the eyepiece and opened his eye so wide that he felt the tip of his lashes brush against the skin above the eyelid. He was trying to imagine the houses, the buildings. There must have been streets and sidewalks and fences and gates and trees.

"What happened to it all?" A stronger wind ruffled the surface of the water darkly.

"They bulldozed everything. First time I'd ever seen a tree-dozer. Ever seen a tree-dozer, Sam?"

"No." Sam shook his head slightly, but kept the water in focus.

"Got a claw on it—spiked like a witch's fist. Can tear up the roots."

Suddenly something floated into the edge of the camera frame, abover the water where the lens captured a piece of sky.

"See something?" Gus asked. "Here, let me tip it up for you." He adjusted the angle of the lens. And it was then that Sam saw it clearly. The bird glided into the frame. With wings horizontal and unmoving it soared on an updraft. Deep within, Sam felt a surge. There was no mistaking. It was an eagle.

"You got one," Gus whispered.

Sam was turning the lens slowly to follow its flight. "Do you think it will land here?"

"Don't know. I've got that fresh deer carcass out there. Should be tempting this time of year. He pretty much staying in the frame?"

"Yeah."

"Well, he's probably spotted it. Let's have a look."

"Sure. You going to film this one?" Sam asked as he backed away from the camera.

"Maybe. We'll see." Gus put his eye to the cup. "Yeah. It's a bald. Golden eagles glide with their wings up more toward the sky. Bald eagles keep theirs pretty horizontal. I don't know if it's one from the reintroduction project or not. Here," Gus said. "I think he's probably going to land. You follow him down. You'll get a real good look at him when he comes to breakfast."

Sam crawled to the platform again. The bird had started to circle tightly. Its wings were still spread out but tilted at a new angle below the 180-degree horizontal plane as if it were scooping the air in front of them. The bird hovered for a few moments, then began to descend quickly. The big talons were extended, clawing against the air. The wings beat slowly in large strokes to break the forward motion, lacing the air with currents and drafts as the immense bird lighted down. The eagle stepped forward, its white head eager and curious. The legs, thick and powerful, lifted high as the bird walked toward the bloody deer carcass, white tail feathers sweeping behind. There was no sky, no water, just this bird filling the frame. In its wind-ruffed cloak of dark feathers, it came forward like a prince.

FIVE

They hiked out in the early morning. For a mile or so they followed the remnants of an old road. The road had once been the main highway linking the valley to other towns. Its blacktop surface was now broken and overgrown. Creeping tree roots had pushed through the surface, and beaver ponds had flooded out many parts of it. Then there was a four-mile hike through the woods, and on snowshoes it took almost two hours. Sam was faster than Gus, who, as he put it, had to pace himself these days.

"You skitter on up there, Sam. Don't worry about me. Keep your eyes open. You might see a flying squirrel."

"Skitter" was hardly the word, Sam thought, as he trudged ahead on the snowshoes. He wasn't sure exactly what was wrong with Gus, but he knew it was something more than old age that was causing him to pace himself.

Hadn't Cousin Leo said something about chemotherapy? Gus had a deep, hacking cough, and as far as Sam could see he was not a smoker. Sam had spent more than twelve hours with him in this accidental wilderness, more time than he had ever spent alone with anyone other than his parents. It seemed odd, being so far away from everything familiar. It was a nice feeling, too—just the two of them, suspended in the isolation of a wilderness.

Sam was sweating hard now. He spotted a log a few yards away and sat down on it to rest and wait for Gus. For a full minute his ears were filled with the sounds of his own body working—his breathing, his blood roaring like white water through a canyon. As his breathing quieted he was startled to realize why his own sounds had been so loud. He sat now in the center of a vast stillness that loomed up and around him like one giant shimmering bubble, fragile and full of light. Gus caught up and sat down beside him on the log. Neither of them spoke. Fifteen minutes later they walked through the wire fencing of gate eleven, the entrance nearest to the blind, and got into Gus Early's car. Gus turned on the engine, backed around, then swung out onto Route 122 and headed toward New Salem.

"They make good pies here. I recommend them highly," Gus said, slipping into the stained-pine booth.

"Pies for breakfast?"

"Sure. Used to eat a whole one every morning."

"A whole pie? Wow!"

"Can't do that anymore, but I'll split one with you—unless you're one of those more traditional bacon-and-eggs types."

"No, not really," Sam said, reflecting briefly on the

volume of Pop-Tarts he had consumed for breakfasts in his lifetime.

"Good." Gus called over to a woman behind the counter. "Mildred? One apple pie—two forks. One coffee." He turned to Sam. "What do you take to drink?"

"Milk will be fine."

"And a glass of milk," Gus added.

Mildred came over carrying a hot apple pie in her mitted hands. She was wearing a heavy sweater under her apron, leg warmers, and knickers. Her gray hair was twisted into a thick bun. Her cheeks were bright pink and she looked like some confection from her own oven. "Cold this morning, Gus. Six below when I got up." Sam had noticed that people in the rural Northeast talked a lot about the weather, much more than Midwesterners did.

"Not too cold for mid-March," Gus responded as he carefully cut the pie down the middle. He then traced the line with his knife tip. "That's your half, Sam. This is mine. No trespassing. Good fences make good neighbors, as they say. Dig in."

"Pretty cold, Gus, even for March," Mildred said from behind the counter. "Last time it was below zero on March 12 was five years ago. Then it was just minus three. Got it in my diary. 1948, now that year it got down to fifteen below. I remember that 'cause I'd just had Tad, and Junior went out to milk the cows and left a pail for the barn cat and it froze up. Junior came in and said to that little red-faced infant nursing there, 'Barn Cat's milk frozed up'—we never did have fancy names for animals round our place, just called them what they were—anyhow, he said, 'Tad, you're lucky yours don't come in pans like Barn Cat's!' " Mildred laughed a cozy morning laugh. Gus joined her. Sam would have laughed harder but was too embarrassed. Mildred had picked up a pie cutter and was gesturing with it toward Gus. "And that was before all this sex-education-in-the-classroom business."

"Don't wave that thing at me, Mildred. I'm educated."

"Well, did you get it in the classroom?" she asked.

"Got it anywhere I could," Gus chuckled, then turned to Sam. "You never come in here and just have a piece of pie and some light conversation, mind you. Not when Mildred is on."

"Which is all the time," she called over the glass pie-display box. "I can't keep help. At least not longer than eight weeks. All these kids over at the college drop out for a quarter and then go back—junior quarter abroad at Mildred's!"

"Maybe you should teach sex in the restaurant—more interesting."

"They don't need any lessons, Gus, believe me." She turned to Sam "Now what do you think, young man? You're in high school."

"Yes," Sam replied cautiously.

"Well, do you think they should teach that stuff?"

"Well, I don't know. I guess it doesn't really bother me."

"They do teach it, then?" Mildred's eyes widened.

"A little in health class."

"Health?" Gus set down his coffee cup. "Why health? I don't see the connection."

"Must be they don't want them to get venereal diseases," Mildred said with authority.

"Oh." Gus took another bite of pie. "Kind of a negative attitude toward the whole thing."

"Well, I for one don't believe it should be taught in

the classroom. That goes for prayer too. I don't believe in school prayer."

"At least you're consistent."

"Is that all you can say about me, Gus? I'm consistent? Want some more coffee?"

"Yes. Yes to the coffee, that is. No, I can think of a lot of things to say about you."

"Maybe you better not." Mildred laughed as she came over with the coffee. "It's just comforting to know that I'm more things than consistent." She smiled at Sam.

"When's spring going to be here?" Sam said suddenly.

Mildred looked directly at him. "Trying to switch the conversation from sex education?" She laughed. "I don't blame you. Are you from around here?"

"Oh, sorry," Gus said, "I didn't introduce you, Mildred. This is Sam, Sam Brooks. Sam, Mildred Dawson. Sam just moved here from the Midwest."

"Well, Sam, pleased to meet you. Now about spring. It's kind of a sore subject around here. Certainly not one of those real consistent things you can count on—speaking of consistency. Sometimes it sort of lurches in with a couple of storms about mid-April. Other years we just slide sweltering and cussing into summer without so much as a daffodil to mark the change. You get used to that."

"Well, Groundhog Day has come and gone long ago."

"Son." Mildred rested her hand lightly on Sam's shoulder. "Groundhog Day is a cruel joke around here, I am sorry to say. Now back in Enfield . . ." Her eyes clouded for a moment. She swallowed quickly. "Back in the valley seems like things did come more or less on schedule. I was looking in my diary the other day, and three years running—1928, '29, '30—we did have crocuses by March 21." Sam was amazed. Mildred did not seem that old.

"You must have started that diary young."

"Six years old—first grade—soon as I learned how to write. My first entry read 'Hot 101 degrees.' I kept that up for a couple of weeks or so. Then I learned how to write two new words: 'Indian summer.' That was back in 1926." She paused. "Seemed like it was always Indian summer then." She turned away briskly and walked back to the counter. Some new customers had just come in.

"So what you doing out this morning, Gus, eagle watching?" A man with a knit cap turned toward them.

"Yep."

"See anything?"

"One bald."

"You see where the QUORP folk are gearing up for another meeting?" Mildred asked.

"Yes, ma'am."

"What you think they're planning to do?" she asked Gus.

"Plan. That's what they're paid to do."

"I swear, Gus, talking to you sometimes is like talking to one of those durned riddling sphinxes. I mean what kind of plans are they making?" Mildred said while delivering coffee to the new customers.

"Turn it into a ski resort, I hear," said one of the men at the counter.

"Now Tillman," Mildred said, "how'd you know a thing like that?" She set down a plate of eggs with ham.

"Hearsay."

"Hearsay—hmmph!" Mildred grunted. "I want to hear Gus-say. He's the one closest to the source down there at the Wildlife Division.

"I haven't heard," Gus said, taking another bite of pie. "Here, you finish it, Sam."

"I'll be trespassing," Sam said, his fork ready.

"It's okay."

The man in the cap, sitting next to Tillman, turned and spoke. "Now Gus, you know how I feel about all this, but you can't tell me that if they just open that northeast corner to limited recreation it's going to upset the applecart and wreck anything."

"Depends on what you think of as the applecart," Gus said, getting up slowly and digging into his back pocket for his wallet.

"The sphinx speaks on," Mildred muttered.

"You get people in there—doesn't have to be a polluting kind of thing like snowmobiles or speedboats—just people on cross-country skis or in canoes. Once you open it up for recreation, you'll get busloads of people coming in from New York, Boston, Connecticut, and you'll lose the eagles. I know. They won't stay."

He walked out, Sam following. "Took us long enough to get any back," Gus whispered hoarsely.

Sam hadn't dared to ask Gus too much about the eagles. In fact, after they had left the blind, Gus had not really talked much about the one they had seen. It was as if, once beyond gate eleven, talking too much about the Quabbin might in some way diminish what was there.

SIX

Dear Gram and Grandpa,

It's spring here, although you'd never guess it. It's funny what they call spring in New England. I think it just means the snow melts but it's still cold and wet, and you can't even count on that. Last Tuesday, April 4, there was a snowstorm. They closed school. They shut down school for anything around here. I guess they don't have the snowplows here that they do in Indiana. Also, all the roads are narrow and hilly and twisty, so they must be hard to clear. Nothing lies flat or straight around here. It takes some getting used to. (I'll never get used to this place, Sam was thinking, but not writing. Who would?)

I'm adjusting. (That's not the same as "getting used to" Sam thought, but it was a good word to use with grandparents.) I am functioning in school. (He had managed to function two A's and two B's on his third-quarter marks. But he had not managed to function any friendships.) Mom is real good. She has a focus now. (Wish I had a focus, Sam thought as he wrote—had one or was one.) She is restoring our house, which is what you do when you buy a historical wreck and not just a plain wreck.

Grandfather Eastman had a small stroke last week. Don't get alarmed. Nobody else is. He has several minor strokes a month. They just readjust his medicine. It's hard talking to him because his speech is slurred. But Grandma Eastman spends two hours a day reading to him. She's a very tough Yankee lady, Mom says. I don't see much difference between a tough Yankee lady and a tough Hoosier one. I think you're every bit as tough, Gram. I couldn't believe that letter last month when you told me about pulling calves in the middle of the night in February—what with Lucas and a broken arm and two cows with complications in forty-eight hours, and a blizzard to boot. What timing! as Mom says.

Mom isn't the only one with a focus. I've got one too—haying. I'll be back mid-June. Schools around here get out late, but Mom says I can leave a week early to help you. So be seeing you in approximately sixty-one days, twelve hours, and forty-two minutes—I checked the airline schedule. There's a noon flight from Boston to Indianapolis stopping in Cincinnati. US AIR flight number 82 leaves Boston 12:00 noon, arrives Cincinnati 2:37. Departs Cincin-

nati 3:05, arrives Indianapolis 3:32 PM. See you
then.

Love, Sam

P.S. I'm going with this man Gus to look for
eagles tomorrow morning. We have to walk into
the place at night so the eagles won't see us
coming. Chances of seeing an eagle around here
are better than seeing a daffodil in May. Crazy
place we moved to.

The night began where the mud left off. The sounds
that Sam heard for the first mile were his own—the suck
of his boots on the wet earth, his own breathing, deep
but not so labored now as in March when they had
snowshoed in. Moonless and black as a tarpot, sky and
earth were one this evening; but gradually, as Sam's eyes
grew used to the night, the dark embroidery of the forest
began to emerge. The frail, naked limb of a tree reached
darkly across the night. Evergreen fronds webbed with
needles floated like huge black snowflakes in the chill
spring night. The tightly spiraled heads of ferns bowed
on serpentine necks. Like miniature dragons they grazed
on mud and darkness, tossing their heads in the light
wind. It was a night forest with black-on-black designs,
laced with dark configurations and intricate shadows.

They reached the blind within an hour. Gus took off
his backpack, reached in and drew out a large, heavily
wrapped package. "Fresh road kill," he said.

"Road kill?" Sam asked.

"Deer run over on Route 122. We take 'em down to
the freezer at the commission. This is just part of a
hindquarter. Eagles like meat with a little fur on it occasionally. Mostly they eat fish, but if any of the old
wintering fellows are still around they might like a little

of this." He was unwrapping the package now. "We'll put it right here in camera range." He walked twenty feet out from the blind, directly in front of the hidden window, and put the joint on the ground. "Can you get me some of that birdseed? It's just inside the door of the blind on the left."

Sam came back with the birdseed. "Why do you always put this out? I've been wondering," he said as Gus scattered some of the seed around.

Gus laughed. "Took me awhile to figure out this trick. The eagles used to come for the meat, but they'd spot the camera lens as soon as I moved it."

"Really?"

"Listen, they can spot a postage stamp from five hundred feet up, so this lens was nothing. Anyway, I got the idea of putting seed out to attract smaller birds. The smaller birds hopping around made a flutter, provided a kind of distraction as well as a screening effect between the eagle and the camera. Nothing I couldn't shoot through, but just enough to camouflage me."

"Can't they smell you?"

"No. Eagles have a lousy sense of smell. Vision. That's their sense. They are the champion visual animal."

They had been inside the blind less than an hour when the first silver winked across the still, black waters of the reservoir. Sam looked through the camera lens. "Moon's coming up," he said.

"Full one, it'll be. Another half hour, this whole forest will be bright with moonlight. Better get some rest, though, before morning."

Sam was about to ask Gus what time it was, but Gus never seemed to wear a watch. He reached for a flashlight to look at his own watch. He beamed the light on it.

"Huh." Sam looked at his watch, perplexed.

"Huh, what?" asked Gus.

"My watch. Must have stopped."

"What do you want to know the time for? Got a date?" Gus chuckled.

"No. Just wondered."

"Never seemed to me that clock time was that much to wonder about."

That was all Gus said—he rarely came out with a word extra. But his silences were never hollow, and his stillness was comforting, somehow. The moonlight was bright now and filtered through some of the small openings in the blind. Gus sat very still, Sam watching him. Clock time did seem meaningless, suddenly. A human's life, after all, was measured in decades; a star's, in millions of years. Compared to a star's the human's life-span was that of a summer gnat. But time could slow down, Sam thought, remembering talks he had had with his father. There was all that speed-of-light theorizing in which star travelers barely aged while earthbound people grew old and died. When the star traveler returned, young and smooth, it was to a world he no longer knew.

By six o'clock the sun was up and by eight they had spotted an eagle circling.

"She's seen it. I'm sure." Gus was referring to the deer meat.

"How do you know it's a she?" Sam asked.

"Don't. Almost impossible to tell except surgically. Females are usually larger, though."

This one was looking fairly large to Sam as it tightened its spiraling course over the meat. Once more the air began to stir. The large wings scooped forward.

"It's a she," Gus said quietly. "Got to be when it's that size."

Sam backed away from the camera so Gus could begin filming. "You do it," Gus said.

"Me?"

"Yeah, you."

"I don't know how to operate this thing."

"Time you learned. The firing button is here." Gus handed Sam a triggering cable that was attached to the camera. "Keep your other hand on those rings on the lens. Those are your zoom and focusing controls. Clockwise zooms in close. Counterclockwise backs off. You're at midrange right now. If the eagle raises its head, come in for a close-up. Try focusing on the eye. It's all in the eye." Gus paused. "It's that eye!" There was a whispered excitement in his voice.

For the first few minutes Sam felt quite stiff with the camera, stiff and awkward. "Don't worry about the camera," Gus whispered. "You're not going to break it. Watch the bird, Sam. Watch it. Let your hands follow what you see."

At first what Sam saw, the movement, seemed like broad, abrupt chunks of motion as the eagle tore at the deer flesh with talons and beak; but he then began to notice a smaller order of movements of the head that seemed separate from those involved in eating and more related to hearing or attention.

"What's that?" Sam whispered suddenly.

"What?"

"Just a second." He waited for it to happen again. He had, he thought, seen a bright gold flash in the eagle's eye. "There!" He said excitedly. Again the eye had flickered as if for a fraction of a second a bright gold disk had slid across it. "The eye—it turned kind of gold for a second."

"The nictitating membrane," Gus whispered. "Third eyelid, they call it. Clears off the cornea. Kind of like a little windshield wiper. Useful when the bird's flying into head winds.

Sam zoomed in briefly for that trillionth of a second when the eagle's eye glinted bright as a tiny westering sun. Then the iris cleared and that remarkable visual intelligence filled the eye again.

It seemed more to Sam than just a visual intelligence. The eagle was suddenly fully alert. Head turned away from the meat, its wings began to fan out. It's going, Sam thought. And within three seconds the bird had lifted from the ground.

"Heard something," Gus said as he watched Sam tilting the lens upward to follow the flight. Within a minute Sam and Gus heard the sounds too—voices and feet in the woods. "Let's see what it is" Gus peered through the lens of the still camera that was to the left of Sam. "Ah! Kids from the Belchertown Home. I forgot they were on the schedule for a hike in here today."

Looking through his own lens, Sam detected something odd about the group. They seemed to lurch rather than move steadily through the woods. They made sounds— not loud ones, but the voices seemed garbled, some deep and throaty, others thickly nasal. Three adults accompanied the group, holding their hands, guiding them, urging them on.

"Who are they?" Sam said softly.

"Kids from the home."

"What home? What kind of home?"

"Belchertown Home for the Homeless. The kids have all sorts of problems—some are mentally retarded, some crippled, some have cerebral palsy. Some I guess are normal, but homeless—so how normal can that be?"

Sam had almost forgotten about his and Gus's invisibility within the blind. They were both following the group with their lenses. Sam had just finished panning from the left to the right when there was a dark, fluid movement in the extreme left of the frame's view. He half expected to see the wings of a bird, not landing, but smooth in flight, gliding on a wind current. It was, however, no winged creature. It was a girl. She walked, then stopped, centered in the lens. She had thick black curly hair; in the light morning breeze it blew across her face like dark storm clouds. Her body, although still, seemed full of music. There was a wild grace about her. She was, Sam thought, the wildest creature in this woods, the wildest living thing he had ever seen. She began to walk on.

Sam followed her with the lens. It was not just the way in which the girl moved that made her different from the others. It was something else. She had a keenness about her. She seemed alert and attuned, not to the woods or the people just ahead of her, but to some other thing entirely. She made no sound, but Sam was sure that when she did her voice would be rich and dark like the notes from a woodwind instrument.

She had no visible physical affliction. Yet she had a strangeness about her that was more complex, more confounding than any physical handicap, any mental retardation that Sam could remember seeing. Moving within her own harmonies, she seemed wrapped in some kind of translucent veil that totally separated her from this world.

"She's a strange one," Gus said, as the girl moved out of the frames of both their lenses.

"Wait!" Sam said. "She's coming back. The group must have gotten ahead of her." Sam began now to turn the zoom mechanism on the camera. He wanted a closer look at the girl, but the image kept blurring. With his left hand he rotated the ring slightly, but still the image kept blurring. "She's coming here! Right here!" he whispered. The girl was indeed walking directly toward them, not just toward the blind but toward the middle window.

"Well, I'll be!" Gus was whispering too. Sam heard the crackling of twigs underfoot and then suddenly there were no trees, no sky, just a dark winking light and then the lens was filled with a luminous jade green eye. Sam pressed his own eye hard against the eyecup and the light from that jade eye came like the flicker of stars in a distant galaxy.

SEVEN

"First time in twenty years," Gus muttered as they crawled out of the blind. "First time anybody ever guessed that this was anything but an abandoned beaver lodge." He straightened up as he came out of the blind. Sam followed and they walked to where the girl was standing. "So, dear, you win the prize!" he said, chuckling warmly. But the girl did not seem to hear him. Gus inclined his head toward her. "Honey?" He paused, "You need help? You lost?" She made no movement, no sound. A dark panic welled up inside Sam. What was wrong with her? Why was she so still, so silent? She seemed to look through them as if they were inanimate objects, perhaps lenses themselves.

"Here you are!" A voice cut the air and a man jogged up behind them. "I'll be! You got us all worried, wandrin' off like that." He reached for her elbow and pulled her.

"C'mon now!" Then he turned to Sam. "She don't talk. Don't let it bother you none." Everything seemed oddly turned around to Sam. Why was this person concerning himself with Sam's feelings? It seemed desperately apparent that it was the girl who needed the concern. She was very pretty, really. Her large green eyes, fringed with dark lashes, dominated her face. She had high, rounded cheekbones and a delicately angled jaw. Her chin seemed a bit too pointed for a dimple, but indeed there was one, and Sam wondered if she might have other dimples if she smiled. But did she ever smile? Her face seemed utterly devoid of any expression. She wore a torn and faded cardigan sweater over a white shirt with an open collar. Just beneath her throat, in that bony hollow at the confluence of neck and collarbone, there was a tarnished locket. Once, probably, it had been shiny silver, but now it was so dark with age it appeared almost black. "C'mon, gal." The man pulled again on her arm, and the girl walked stiffly off, a step behind him.

"Gal?" called Sam. "Is that her name—Gal?"

"No." The man turned as he walked. "Lucy. Lucy Swift." Sam stood very still as he watched them go, so still it was as if he did not want to disturb anything around him, not one molecule or atom which might bear some trace of the girl's strange presence. But the music was all gone. Her movements were wooden, the fluid grace spent.

When they left through gate eleven, Sam had the same feeling he had experienced on previous visits—that for them to talk about what they had seen would diminish it. Behind gate eleven was the wilderness, the eagle, and now the girl. Her name ran through Sam's head like the tumbling waters of a lively brook. Lucy Swift. He could not forget her eyes—the luminous jade at the far end of the lens.

Mildred set down the pie between them. "Extra whipped cream, Sam?"

"Sure, if you don't mind."

"Nope, not at all."

She went back to the counter. "So tomorrow night's the big meeting, Gus. You going to speak?"

"Guess so. Audubon folks coming up asked me to say a word."

"Well, try for more than just a single word, Gus. I don't like the way this thing is going, you know," she said, walking over with the whipped cream. "There was a helicopter out there two days last week and once the week before. If you ask me . . . "

"I didn't, but go ahead," Gus laughed.

"Well, you know what I think they're doing, Gus?" She pulled up a chair, sat down and rested her elbows on the table. Her ruddy face was knotted with intensity. Deep vertical lines left creases between her eyebrows. "They're photographing just like back in '29 when they were too lazy . . . " She stopped, her mouth tensely set.

"Too lazy?" Sam prompted.

"Too lazy. After they took over the whole valley they were too damn lazy to come out here and assess the houses on site. So they just hired a bunch of photographers to take pictures of the properties. I know. They did it to my folks and Frank's folks. You tell me how you evaluate a house from a photograph. And that's how they're going to size up the what-do-you-call-it?"

"Recreational potential?" Gus offered.

"Before you know it, Gus, your hacking tower's going

to be gone, and Disney World will be there right on the shores of the Quabbin."

"Disney World!" Sam exclaimed midbite.

"Well, maybe not Disney World," Mildred conceded, "but we don't need a whole stream of hikers and skiers coming in."

"Bunch out there today from the Belchertown Home."

"Well, small groups like that, it's okay. Those poor things hardly ever get to see the light of day."

"So, I take it," Gus said, getting up, "that you're going to be at the meeting tomorrow?"

"Darn right."

When Sam arrived home his mother was in the backyard arranging rocks with the aid of a man driving a backhoe. She had decided to create a Japanese-style rock garden in the area behind her study and workroom.

"A little to the left," she shouted, motioning with her hand. "Okay, set it down here now . . . wait, wait! Back another foot. . . ." The chain creaked on the granite boulder. "Hold it right there and don't drop it on my toe." Philippa walked up to the rock, which was suspended eight inches above the ground, and guided it slowly forty-five degrees around. "There, now let it down." She caught a glimpse of her son. "Hi, Sam. Just a little Zen rock rolling going on here."

"That's a neat rock," Sam said, referring to the one just placed.

"Isn't it? Did you see the lichen on the other side?"

"Yeah." Sam looked around. There were six or seven large rocks placed on the shady piece of land. Each rock was unique in its shape. The one the backhoe had just set down had a deep vertical dent in its center. The one next to it with a jagged profile reminded Sam of the spiky back of a stegosaurus. Then there were two low rocks that seemed almost to flow, suggesting rivers and streams.

"It's going to look nice," Sam said.

"You bet. We're talking serious stuff here." Philippa laughed. "We're talking rocks. New England granite."

"What are you going to put in between the rocks?" Sam asked, nodding toward the carefully raked mounds of dark loam.

"Moss. Hair moss—grows in profusion around here."

"Is it that kind that looks like miniature pine trees?"

"Yes. There's a bit over there by the edge of our property." She pointed to a wooded corner of the field that took up where the lawn left off. Sam remembered seeing a lot of it out at the Quabbin. "The landscape man should be here with a truckload any minute."

Any minute stretched into several hours. By the time the truck arrived it was nearly suppertime. "We'll come back tomorrow, Mrs. Brooks, to put it in," the landscaper said.

Sam could tell that his mother was disappointed. Of all the restoration projects so far, the creation of this garden had seemed to excite her the most. He felt sorry for her. She seemed suddenly like a little kid told by grown-ups that she would have to wait "just one more day."

"Well, you're sure you'll be back tomorrow?"

"Bright and early. It doesn't take long to put in. Real easy to do. Just put it down right on top of the loam and tamp it in good and firm with your feet. Water it well. That's all there is to it."

They went inside after the man had left. Philippa walked over to the refrigerator. "Gee, what's for dinner?" she said absently. She turned to Sam. "I was so preoccupied with the darned garden I didn't even think about dinner."

"Improvise, Mom. Anything will do."

"That's what Daddy was good at—improvisation. Remember what he could do with canned pineapple, left-over meat, and a bottle of soy sauce!"

"Ummm," Sam hummed, and silently cursed himself for ever uttering the word *improvise*. Philippa had opened the refrigerator. Hanging on the door, she peered in.

"Speak to me!" she whispered, then turned to Sam. "It's not speaking to me."

"What?"

"The refrigerator. It's not talking."

"What do you want—the Delphic oracle?"

Philippa laughed. "Very good, Sam." A little classical allusion always cheered an English-teacher mother, Sam thought. Philippa had opened the freezer compartment and begun to rummage through. "If we had a microwave I could thaw this pork roast and cook it in five minutes."

"We could drive it over to Aunt Nez's. She's got one."

"That seems excessive." Philippa looked over her shoulder. "Sam, would you think I was a terrible mother if we had Popsicles, ham, and—let's see—frozen peas for dinner?"

"Oh, yeah. I'd call the child-abuse hotline immediately."

"What flavor?"

"Grape, if there're any left."

Philippa got out the box. "How the heck do you tell the flavor of these things? Come to think of it, why has the Popsicle industry never printed the flavor on the wrapper? It seems dumb not to." She tore off the tip of one wrapper. "Ah ha! Grape! First try. Here. I'll take potluck."

A few minutes later Sam and his mother were sitting opposite one another at the kitchen table. On each plate were thin slices of luncheon ham and a mound of peas, on Sam's a grape Popsicle and on his mother's an orange one.

"Well, it's colorful. You can say that for it," Philippa exclaimed. They ate in silence. Sam licked his Popsicle and thought about the strange girl, Lucy Swift, he had met that afternoon. One could hardly say "met." "Encountered" was a more accurate description of what had happened. She must be deaf and dumb, he thought. But that didn't seem right, somehow. He was almost sure she could hear. It was as if what she heard was not being processed. He was just about to ask his mother if she had ever known any deaf people when he noticed how still she had become. Her Popsicle was melting and making a large orange pool on her plate. Her chin rested in her cupped hand. She was thinking about his father. Darn! Why had he said that dumb word? She had been so good these last few months.

"Mom, your ham's going to taste like orange Popsicle."

"Oh." She picked up the stick and the Popsicle dropped off.

"I'll get you another one," he offered quickly.

"Never mind. I'm not really hungry."

He could feel her slipping away from him. "Hey, Mom," he said suddenly. "I got a great idea!"

"What's that?" She was trying to muster some enthusiasm in her voice.

"That guy, the landscape man, said the moss was easy to put in. Why don't we do it tonight? You and me."

A genuine brightness now flooded Philippa's voice.

"What a good idea. I bet we could do it in a couple of hours."

"Let's go!"

They whispered excitedly in the moonlight as they worked.

"It feels great. It's so soft," Sam said.

"But it's quite tough. Smothers weeds. You can stomp on it. Roll on it. When all the baby cousins come over we can put them out here. They'll love it." She paused. "I love it!"

"I like the rocks," Sam said, tamping in some more moss at the base of the flat-topped rock that was just right for sitting. At night the rocks looked different from in full daylight. By day, a large boulder with a rounded top rose like a miniature mountain above the long, flat rock beside it. At night, limned by the moon, it lost its mass and appeared as a kneeling figure beside a stream. An ovalish rock with a hump in the middle now slept like a cat in the shadows in the cover of the broad, dark leaves of a hosta plant. Images slid and imagination wandered in a garden cast with rock shadows and streaked with moonlight.

Even as he worked, Sam could not forget the moment when he had come out of the blind and seen Lucy standing there. Her eyes had been flickering behind the dark tangles of hair and she stood without a sound, yet attuned. He had concentrated on her eyes at the time. They were like no other eyes he had ever seen. It was not just that they were luminous like stars. They were like space and time, woven together to make the single fabric of the universe. To look out into space was to look back in time. Sam heard soft, small sounds around him. At first he had the absurd idea that the moss was crying. But when he turned he saw his mother bent over on her knees, her forehead pressed into a thick patch of moss she had just planted and her shoulders shaking.

"Mom!"

"Oh, Sam, I miss Daddy so much!"

"Oh, Mom!" he crawled over to her and touched her lightly on the shoulder.

She straightened up. "Don't worry. I'll be okay," she said, taking a handkerchief out of her jeans pocket. "It's nothing." She blew her nose. "What do I mean it's nothing! It's the worst thing that's ever happened to us!" She wiped her nose vigorously. "But don't worry. You haven't seen me like this since we've been in New Salem, have you?"

"No, you've been great."

"Too great. I get to cry some now. You go on inside. We're almost done here. I'll finish up."

"I don't mind your crying. I can take it."

"I know. But I just want to do it in private. You've been so good about all this house restoration and garden stuff and me. What a sport. I didn't even ask you how your day was with Gus. We'll talk about it when I come in. Now run along."

Sam got up and went in. She meant well. Sam knew it, and yet those words "run along" brushed away the delicate web of moonlight and night air like a broom's bristles hell-bent on spring cleaning.

EIGHT

"Hello, Gus!" Philippa called across the parking lot as she got out of Mildred Dawson's car in the warm May evening. She and Sam had hitched a ride with Mildred to the recreational-planning meeting.

"Good to see you, Philippa," Gus said as the four of them joined the stream of people filing through the doors of the elementary school.

"Surprised" was more like it, Sam thought—or at least he had been when his mother had suddenly announced that she was coming to the meeting. He had not realized that she was so interested in the QUORP (Quabbin Organization for Recreational Planning) versus QUAVA (Quabbin Valley Association) battle over the future of the Quabbin. There were a lot of people he had not expected to see—his own high-school principal and the rather curious man who owned an antique store in New

Salem and lived with his mother down the street from them. The man's mother, a veritable antique herself, was also there. Sam saw Philippa wave to Leo as she entered the auditorium. Sitting next to him, out of uniform, was the state trooper who hung around the junction of 2A and Route 202 and caught people who did not come to complete a stop.

The auditorium was packed, but Sam and his mother were able to sit together. Gus took a seat in the row just in front of them and Mildred was motioned closer up, where friends had saved her a place. The meeting was called to order. The first ten minutes was boring, but shortly things proceeded to the heart of the conflict.

"There is a road—a broken blacktop road that once was the main highway to Dana and North Dana. That road and the common it led to are overgrown now with brier and goldenrod. When my grandson and I hike in there . . ." The small, neat man was standing in front of a microphone and speaking to the full auditorium. On either side of the podium from which he spoke was a long table. To the left were the men and women from the QUORP. To the right were the board members of QUAVA. "When we go down that weed-clogged avenue that used to be the site of my own father's store, our house, and the homes and businesses of our friends, and I tell my grandson the sad tale of how, fifty years before, his great-grandfather and great-grandmother and countless others were pushed out, about how all the engineers with fancy degrees from Harvard and Massachusetts Institute of Technology came up here and did their planning to quench the thirst of the city folk down in Boston that resulted in our losing our homes, farms and businesses"—his voice began to rise—"and dug up our dead!" He paused. "Well, I say we should at least have access—a little more access—to the Quabbin waters, the very same waters that drowned our past." There was a hearty swell of applause but a fair number of boos. A rather loud boo, Sam noticed, emanated from the area where Mildred was sitting. The man took a seat near Mildred.

"Harry Bingham!" Mildred's voice carried over the rows of seats. "You should be ashamed of yourself. How much water do you need, for Pete's sake?"

"Not for Pete's sake, Mildred. For little Billy's sake. It would make a great swimming hole for kids."

"He can go over to Miller's Pond like my grandchildren. He doesn't need four hundred and twelve billion gallons of water to swim in!"

"Sh! Sh!" People started hushing them.

"You'll get your turn, Mildred," someone called out.

In fact Mildred was the next speaker for QUAVA. She hurried up to the podium.

"Well, hello," she said, then turned to the moderator. "I don't have to be sworn in or anything?"

"It's not a trial," he replied dryly. "We're not looking for guilt or innocence." Everybody laughed.

"Well, I hope you're looking for the truth!" Mildred snapped.

"She's something," Philippa leaned over and whispered to Sam.

"She makes good pies, too," Sam said.

"My name's Mildred Dawson," she continued. "Like Harry Bingham, I came from the valley, not Dana, like Harry, but Enfield. Now my town, Enfield, unlike Dana, is totally underwater. Dana was bought—I'm saying this for the Boston press so they can get their facts straight in the paper—Dana was bought by the Water Commission and officially ceased to exist as a town in 1938—

April 28, to be exact. Buildings were leveled in Dana, but much of the land was left above water. Enfield was another story, as I said, and I for one have no desire to go swimming over my old homesite, school, or church." The people laughed.

"You laugh, but I see no need for others, regardless of their connection with these towns, to open up the waters of the Quabbin for recreation, swimming, or more fishing and boating. What is now open for recreational purposes is sufficient. I'm not an old stick-in-the-mud either. I like to play as much as the next person. But there are plenty of other places around here to hike, fish, or swim. The Quabbin is one of the cleanest water supplies in the country, I'm told. We have wildlife there, and the eagles will be coming back to nest. Now, we lost the valley once and it was awful. No one knows it better than I and"—she raised her finger and shook it toward the audience—"and Harry, you should know that too! But the valley came back to us—maybe not in a better way, but certainly in an unexpectedly good way." She paused and took a deep breath. "We can't bring back the past, but for all of our sakes let's not lose the valley again. That's all I have to say." She flushed a deep pink and walked off the platform back to her seat.

The next speaker was a woman planner from QUORP.

"I'm Claire Kirk and I'm from Southeastern University where I am an associate professor of planning and land use in the architecture school. Now, my statement is going to be brief. I have listened tonight and . . . " She paused. Her face assumed a slightly pained look. "I want you people to know that I hear you. It is not hard to imagine the anxieties that accompany decisions such as these; but after our three-year study of this area and as a consultant to the master planning committee it is my conclusion that indeed this vast area is to some degree underutilized."

"Land's there, got to use it," muttered Gus.

The woman continued. "To always think that recreation and wilderness are at odds with one another is oversimplifying the case."

"We can have our cake and eat it too?" Gus whispered. "No way."

"With judicious planning, some of the restrictions in the northeast corner could be eased. It is my recommendation that a committee of valley citizens in conjunction with recreation and land-use planners determine the kinds and extent of activities."

The woman talked for another minute. She received warm applause from the room. QUORP was smart to bring her in, Sam thought. She reeked of expertise, and she was a good politician to boot. Sam was shocked to see his mother raise her hand. She had only decided to come at the last minute.

"A question at the back of the room?" the moderator said.

"Yes," Philippa said in a voice that didn't sound much like her own.

Sam was in agony. This could be the most embarrassing moment of his life, he thought.

"I have a question."

"Could you please stand, Miss . . . er . . ."

Terminal embarrassment, Sam thought. I am absolutely going to drop dead right here.

She was saying her name now. "Mrs. Brooks—Philippa Brooks from New Salem. I have just one question for Miss Kirk." Her voice was growing stronger.

"Yes! Yes! Of course." Miss Kirk said, coming back toward the podium.

"Well, I just wondered, Miss Kirk." She just wondered! Sam studied his mother. Her voice was very strong now and there was a determined, indeed almost defiant set to her jaw. "Well, when you say that the Quabbin is to some degree underutilized, what exactly does that mean?"

Gus Early turned around and smiled as broadly as Sam had ever seen. The old English teacher strikes again! The fear and embarrassment drained out of him.

"Underutilized," Philippa continued, "for what, by what, or compared to what?" A ragged cheer went up in the room. Miss Kirk really looked pained now.

"Well, that's a complex question to answer."

"But," the moderator spoke now, "I think it's an important one. Could you try to answer it, Miss Kirk?"

"Well, I think it would take too long to do so here tonight, but I can refer all those who are interested to the third section of the Master Plan Report on Recreational Usage, which gives a series of tables on acreage and per-capita recreational needs of Americans. I'm sure Mrs. Brooks will find these quite fascinating. There are also some interesting correlations between nonpolluting activities such as cross-country skiing and mental health."

Mildred Dawson squirmed in her chair and whispered loudly. "Nobody around here has gone nuts yet 'cause they couldn't cross-country ski on the banks of the Quabbin."

Gus was the final speaker of the evening, and what he said was very brief indeed: "You have heard from several people tonight—experts, residents of old Enfield, Dana, and Prescott, people from the Water Commission. Most of you know who I am. Gus Early. State Division of Fisheries and Wildlife, former Enfielder. Most of you know what a remarkable wildlife area we have at the Quabbin—deer, beaver, red-tailed hawks, flying squirrels, and in the winter it's a feeding ground for eagles. There is even a chance now we might get them back for good. A real nesting and breeding population right here in the state."

"Birds!" Someone called out. "What about people like us!"

The moderator called for order.

"Okay." There was only a slight edge of irritation in Gus's voice. "I've hiked those woods for over fifty years. I know that wilderness and love it. As chief photographer for the Wildlife Division, I photograph it year in and year out. Even if the Quabbin were closed to everyone, including myself—if I could never walk through gate eleven again—I would be completely happy knowing that it was there." He paused. "There and wild and free for the animals—it would never be underutilized!"

They had walked in the door of the restaurant with Mildred. Gus was directly behind him when Sam felt the hand drop hard on his shoulder. "Oh, my God!" Gus seemed to cough the words more than speak them. There was a crash. Sam wheeled around and saw him on the floor.

Mildred acted quickly. Within seconds she had called the emergency number. Although to Sam it seemed like hours, less than ten minutes passed before an ambulance arrived. He vaguely remembered the attendant's saying that Gus's vital signs were stable after Sam and his mother had piled into the ambulance.

Mildred followed in her own car. They were heading south toward Belchertown. "Fifteen minutes—max," the attendant had said it would take. Sam rode in the back with Gus, and as the spinning red lights flashed in the night he could pick out the MDC gates along 122 as they raced toward Belchertown. Gate eleven flashed somberly for a second in the eerie patches of reflected red light.

NINE

"603–27–8508."

"Eight?" his mother asked, bending over the forms that she and Mildred were filling out in the waiting room.

"Yeah—eight-five-zero-eight." Sam repeated the last four digits of Gus's social-security number. To be reciting these numbers seemed like an extraordinarily absurd activity. The sound of his voice saying the nine-digit chain jangled meaninglessly in the room. They were as silly sounding as the nonsense rhymes and invented language Alice encountered when she stepped through the looking glass. What in the world did these numbers have to do with living and dying? There was more paper than medicine to being sick. Maybe it was all designed to distract the family and friends from interfering or becoming hysterical. But there was no way not to be scared.

Nurses and orderlies came and went from behind the

green door where Gus lay. Sam tried to keep track of their movements. Sometimes the intervals seemed too long, and once when two people had gone in and then immediately came out, he worried that Gus had been left all alone. But the woman at the nurse's station said no, that there was a resident with Gus and that Sam should just go and relax. There was a snack bar on the first floor and a vending machine at the end of the corridor. Sam headed now for the vending machine. He bought a bag of Reese's Pieces and a Coke. Now he could go back and wait some more. He tore open the Reese's Pieces bag and popped the tab on the Coke can. Mildred and his mom continued to wade through the sea of papers.

He tried hard to concentrate on the candy, but his eyes kept swinging toward the green door. At least no "codes" had squawked, or the sound that was supposed to signal cardiac arrest. What was happening to Gus behind that door? Were they pouring radioactive chemicals into his veins? Were there tubes down his throat, or were they cutting a hole in his windpipe? There were no distractions from fear. A nurse came out with a somber look and walked directly toward him. Sam felt awash with dread. He slipped a small piece of candy into his mouth, sucked hard, squashed it between his tongue and the roof of his mouth, and swallowed. Then, in a last-ditch effort to control himself, he began to whisper, " 'Twas brillig and the slivey tove . . .' "

"Are you Sam?" the nurse asked.

"Yes." Mildred and his mom appeared at his side.

"Mr. Early is doing nicely. He's stabilized and will be moved from intensive care within an hour. The rules are that he can only see one visitor at a time, and he's requested to talk to Sam." Sam felt his mother's hand touch him lightly on the elbow.

"So, if you'll just follow me."

He followed. His eyes were riveted on the nurse's white back. The crazy poem rang in his head: "Did gyre and gimble in the wabe. All mimsey were the borogroves. . . ." They went through the green door into a larger area partitioned off by screens. "Beware the Jabberwock, my son. . . ." His dad had been behind one of these screens, covered up entirely—the modesty of death. "The jaws that bite . . ." He wasn't sure he could handle this. It was apparently not a heart attack. "Beware the Jubjub bird, and shun . . ." The nurse pulled the drapery screen aside and then she left. Sam looked after her in alarm. Slowly, he turned to the bed.

"Hi," Sam said softly as he peered through the network of tubing. There was a little tube in Gus's nose and one in each wrist. Bottles and bags of colorless fluid hung in seeming precariousness above, as gravity and chemicals did whatever they were supposed to do to sustain life. Sam's concentration struggled through the jungle of plastic vines toward Gus. He looked a lot better already, Sam thought. Maybe it was just a severe fainting spell. Or maybe it was just a bad dream that Sam was going through, the kind he had had so often months before when he would wake up expecting to find out that a terrible mistake had been made. Or maybe it should be called a wonderful mistake, for his father had not been killed after all, and everything was all right, like before. There was no "like before," however, with Gus. Their friendship had just begun. They were in the process of making the "like before." It wasn't fair. He looked at the old man's face. There were all sorts of lines, fine ones thin as the filaments of a spider's web, sun-squinting creases that flared out from the eyes, which were now closed. Sam half believed that when those eyes opened he might see, in that first fraction of a second, the bright gold disk that had flashed across the eye of the eagle.

It wasn't fair; and then again, why did he even care? Sam suddenly remembered the old story his mother had read him as a child. It was one of his favorites, about the boy named Pierre who never cared and finally, because he never cared, was eaten by a lion. There was a funny phrase about how the boy was not really dead but was somehow shaken out of the lion. He could not remember the exact words now, but they were always twisted through the dream about his father, those aching dreams in which it was all a terrible mistake and nobody was really dead.

Gus opened his eyes and lifted his hand from the bedcovers. "Listen to me, Sam."

"Maybe you shouldn't talk now."

"Listen!" Gus turned his head toward Sam. "In a few minutes a doctor's going to come in here and say, "How are we doing?" or some garbage like that, and tomorrow they'll be doing some tests on me." Sam bit his lower lip. He didn't want to hear this. He really was frightened now, but he tried not to let it show. He even smiled a little. But maybe Gus couldn't see his smile through the tubing that came right across his line of vision. "They don't have to do tests. I know it's back." A bunch of little no's crowded in Sam's throat. He swallowed them back. Gus looked hard at Sam. "You're scared. I can see it. You don't have to put on any nice face for me, Sam. It's all right." He paused. "You know what I'm talking about? Cancer. I knew it—the cancer—would come back. In the next couple of days I've got some real decisions to make."

"What kind of decisions do you mean?"

Gus exhaled. There was a small rasping sound. "Time-buying ones." He opened his eyes wide and raised an eyebrow. "That might seem a little selfish to some. I've had seventy-six great years. But I want to negotiate for a few more months."

"Negotiate with whom?" Sam asked.

Gus laughed at this. "With me, of course." Then he looked sharply at Sam. "Look, I don't mean to shock you. I'm no atheist. I don't go to church, but I do believe." Sam saw the belief. Gus's eyes were a faded brown, but sharp. Sam saw more belief in the old man's gaze than he had in a year of Sundays in the church in Kokomo. "But this cancer business at my age is not between me and God or me and doctors."

Sam nodded.

"I'm not the kind to go whining around to God for more—that would be, as they say, looking a gift horse in the mouth." Sam was sure that although Gus was not an atheist his brand of religion was certainly unique. "No," Gus continued. "At my age the cancer is between me and me, or me and those cells in me that are going haywire. I've got to buy some time and I've got to figure out how much I can take in terms of the chemotherapy and radiation. I don't mind feeling sick for four weeks if it will buy me four months. But if four weeks just gets me five weeks . . ."

"What do you mean?" Sam whispered.

"It makes you sick, sick as a dog."

"Four weeks gets you five?" Sam asked confusedly.

"Come closer, Sam," Gus said after a minute. Sam walked around the stand from which the bag of clear fluid was suspended. Close up the view was different— Gus's cheeks were a bit more concave, his mouth unusually taut. "Look," Gus whispered. His voice was tired. "I'll even settle for three months. That would include going to Manitoba for the eaglets and seeing them through their release. It's also when the final vote will come in on the QUORP master plan. So you get the picture, Sam?"

"Yes, sir," he spoke very softly, then watched Gus's hand as it patted his own. There was a tiny needle taped into the vein, some dried blood around the tape.

"Didn't mean to put all this on you." It was as if the hand were talking, gentle despite the needle. "But I figure you should know, us spending all that time together and all out there in the blind. Go over there, Sam." He gestured toward a chair with his trousers on it. Sam got up. "In the right-hand pocket are the keys to gate eleven and to the blind. Get a duplicate set made for yourself."

"Me?"

"Yes, you. We've got to have footage, Sam, of the birds. Talk like tonight's is cheap, but if we can show that the bald eagles are coming back as a breeding population—well, hell, nobody's going to evict the national bird."

"And you think *I* can do the filming?"

"You've got to. I'm going to be out of commission for a while. That big eagle we saw the day before yesterday was brought in and released four years ago. It's been back twice now this spring and once last year. They nest in their fourth or fifth year. We have a chance with this one."

Sam stared hard at Gus. He could not say anything. He should feel honored, but all he could feel was incompetent and scared. He had operated the camera only once.

"I don't even know how to load the camera, Gus."

"No problem. I'll have Steve from the department bring one over here tomorrow and I'll show you myself.

These are just problems, Sam. Problems can be solved." Gus's voice had grown steadily weaker. "Now you better get on home. See you tomorrow."

A few minutes after Sam had left and the doctors had come and gone, Gus managed to raise himself up on his elbow. The bed was close to a window overlooking the street. He saw Sam and Sam's mother and Mildred standing by the curb. The two women's heads were bent toward one another in conversation. Sam stood off a few feet looking diagonally across the street at the Belchertown Home for the Homeless. What was it that he had said to the boy, something about all the time they had spent together in the blind? He should have just said it was special. Too bad he was so tight-lipped—not enough time to learn different. Hardly enough time to get out to Manitoba.

He sank back on the bed and closed his eyes. Maybe the blind was becoming a hacking ground of sorts for the quiet boy from Kokomo. What a funny-sounding name for a town, he thought, and fell asleep. The nurse came in to check him. "He likes flat," Gus mumbled.

"What?" the nurse asked and leaned over to hear better. But Gus didn't hear her. He was dreaming—a funny dream of a winged boy flying over cornfields in Kokomo, Indiana.

Sam stood on the curb with Philippa while Mildred went to get her car. For some minutes he had been staring at the building across the street without really seeing it. Now suddenly the words over the entrance stood in stark relief against the brick. BELCHERTOWN HOME FOR THE HOMELESS. The girl in the woods—Lucy Swift—she was inside that building! The thought was somehow profoundly disturbing. But at that same moment he

started to laugh, for the words from the book came back
to him now:

> They rushed the lion
> into town.
> The doctor shook him
> up and down.
> And when the lion
> gave a roar—
> Pierre fell out
> upon the floor.
> He rubbed his eyes
> and scratched his head
> and laughed
> because he wasn't dead.

TEN

By the time they reached home it was past midnight. Once Sam was upstairs, alone in his room, he felt better. The manic desire to laugh had subsided. He got undressed and went to bed, thinking of Lucy Swift, wondering if he might ever see her again. He imagined her walking, wooden and detached, through the long corridors of the Belchertown Home. Then she was moving through the woods near the blind just as he had first seen her in the camera lens. Images whirled through his head. That darn camera. Would he ever get any decent footage? What if he blew it? He could just imagine it— a record of a dwindling species, overexposed, bleached white, because of his goofing up. A wilderness's only shot at remaining wild lost because the only pictures of . . . ! He couldn't think of it now. He was becoming overwhelmed by images of his own incompetence.

Above his bed where the skylight framed the night, the moon transcribed an arc as it passed to the edge of the frame. Sam threw off his covers. "Can't sleep!" he muttered. He walked over to the window seat opposite his bed. Looking out he saw his mother in the Japanese garden. She was kneeling in a column of moonlight. Her thin white nightgown blew around her body like mist. She was planting something. Or maybe she was placing the small, smooth river stones he had helped her collect a few weeks before. He watched his mother bending, curving close to the earth as she went about arranging a kind of beauty, ordering a kind of growth.

Gus too was devoted to ordering a kind of growth. Three months was all that he asked for. Three months to try and shore up a species with a fifty-million-year history, more than ten times that of man. Sam continued to look down at the moon-washed garden. The sky just overhead was clear, but clouds were rolling up, and beyond the garden everything seemed to disappear into a fuzzy darkness. The borders between lawn and field, field and woods, had dissolved. Beyond the woods were gates twenty-eight and twenty-nine, which led into the Quabbin. Perhaps this garden, bright with moonlight, was like a star in the blackness of the country beyond. Perhaps light from the garden went out as if it were a distant star, light-years away. Would its light reach the gates? "No," whispered Sam. If we are a star, he thought, then the Quabbin, with its lost villages, is a black hole in the heavens. His father had told him about black holes. They occurred where a star collapsed upon itself and sank inward, pulling all matter with it, even light. The gravity of a black hole was so strong that not a single ray of light could escape. None of the ordinary laws of physics applied to black holes. His father had described them as little rips in the fabric of space and time. They were invisible, detectable only because of their effects on companion stars.

As Sam looked down, the garden seemed to grow brighter. His mother continued her ordering. She laid a cupped hand on a small, rounded stone as if it were as fragile as a newborn's skull. One must not think of black holes, Sam thought, for the death of a star was a sad and scary thing. He remembered something else his father had said: that there was a time before the stars, before the universe, when mass and energy were one, and there was simply no way to define time. It was a time just before the beginning of time.

ELEVEN

THIS ENTRANCE NO LONGER IN USE. ALL VISITORS PLEASE USE SPRING ST. ENTRANCE. The windows on the double doors had been painted black. Sam went quickly back down the concrete stairs, turned left and left again to Spring Street. A new wing of glass and steel had been grafted onto the old brick building. Nothing had been done architecturally to ease the transition from old to new—not even a token brick used decoratively in the sidewalk or facade. The old part wouldn't win any beauty prizes, however, Sam thought as he walked through the doors of the new wing the sign proclaimed to be the Arthur and Janet Hubbell Wing of the Belchertown Home for the Homeless.

Sam stepped into a pool of bright light. The strong midday sun poured through several skylights and large floor-to-ceiling windows, bouncing off the chrome furniture and pale linoleum floors. For a split second Sam was engulfed in a white blindness and could not see or move.

"Can I help you?" The woman's voice melted out of the platinum light.

"Oh, yes." Sam moved toward the white and chrome desk. Shards of light sliced through the air, crisscrossing, bouncing, fracturing the space around him. He felt as if he were caught in a noiseless cross fire. Three flat pastel sunspots floated across the woman's face. She was wearing sunglasses. "The light's murder in here this time of day. A million-dollar wing and they make a big boo-boo like this." She gestured toward the bank of windows. "They're coming to treat the glass next week, though. What can I do for you?"

"I'd like to visit Lucy Swift."

"Lucy Swift," the woman said vaguely, as if trying to place her. "Oh, Lucy Swift, of course!" She paused and leaned forward as if to see him better. Sam expected her to take off her glasses, but she didn't. "Why are you here to see Lucy, of all people?"

Of all people, Sam thought. Why did the woman say that? He was oblivious now to the frantic play of light around the woman. "Well, because I know her."

"You know her!" There was a near hoot of disbelief in the woman's voice.

"Yes," Sam replied quietly.

"But nobody knows Lucy. She can't talk. Has never talked in all the years she's been here."

The shards of light had stilled, but the flattened colored bubbles edged toward the rim of Sam's vision. He concentrated hard on the woman. She had just delivered her pronouncements on Lucy with a small smile that, although not smug, was rather cold in its calculated tenderness. Darn the sunspots! Sam blinked fiercely. "She's my friend," Sam said, lifting his chin a bit and looking at the woman levelly, ignoring the two black disks that shielded her eyes.

Again the tender calculation. "But she has no friends."

"She has me." He stepped forward. "I want to see her, please," he said, leaning slightly over the desk and looking directly through the woman's dark lenses. He could just barely make out her eyes. They appeared slightly startled.

"I'll see what I can do!" she said quickly, and got up.

A few minutes later she returned. With her was a nurse in a white uniform, cap, running shoes and sunglasses. "So you want to see Lucy?" Either Sam was getting better at this or the nurse's tea-colored lenses allowed him to see her eyes better. He did feel, however, that he was talking with a more complete person. "Are you a relative?" she asked.

For a brief moment Sam thought maybe he should lie and say he was. "Well," he paused, "no, no. I'm a friend. I can't understand what the problem is. Why can't I see her?"

"Well," said the nurse, turning to the other woman and resting a hand on her hip. "I guess there's no law against this. It's not like we're giving a controlled substance without a prescription. Come along." She had turned to lead the way out of the lobby toward a corridor. "There's nothing on Lucy's chart that says she can't see a friend." And then in a lower voice she added, "There's nothing really on Lucy's chart at all." She looked over her shoulder at Sam. "Follow me."

They walked through a corridor with a ceiling of curved glass. It was like passing through a tube of light.

The place must have been designed by laser freaks, Sam thought, squinting against the new ambush of light. The nurse looked back over her shoulder and saw Sam fighting the glare. "You don't have any sunglasses, huh?"

They should provide them, Sam was thinking. Fit you at the front door just like in *The Wizard of Oz*. Dorothy, Toto, the Tin Woodman—the whole crew got them at the gate to the Emerald City to shield their eyes from the green glare. Sam and the nurse turned a corner, and the intense light seemed to retreat a bit.

"Okay." The nurse shoved her glasses up into her curly mop of reddish hair. Her face was freckled and slightly plump. She had light gray eyes. "Now, what's your name?"

"Sam—Sam Brooks."

"Okay, Sam. Why don't you go through that blue door. Second one down. It's a lounge. I think Lucy will be comfortable there. I'll go fetch her. I think probably we'll have to have an attendant with her."

"Attendant? Why? Is she violent or something?"

"Oh, heavens no. It's just that, well . . ." The nurse's lips pursed. "I really don't know why exactly, except Lucy's never had a visitor and I think if anything did happen . . . for your own sake."

It amazed Sam that people connected with Lucy seemed to be more concerned with his welfare than with hers. "Okay," he said quickly. "I'll wait in the room."

The lounge was also too bright to be comfortable. It was not as bad as the corridor or the lobby, however. Pieces of sunlight lay on the carpet, like shapes from a cookie cutter. The cathedral ceiling had been cut open at various intervals into geometric figures. In the center of the room were two large triangles. Rectangles and disks of light lay around the periphery of the floor. There were some coffee tables and two larger tables, one of which had a partially composed jigsaw puzzle on it. There was a card table with a checkerboard, and magazine racks and a television set. In one corner two couches formed a seating area. Toward the center of the room was an arrangement of three easy chairs. There were also fake-leather beanbag chairs against a wall. Near one table was a box of toys; Sam had noticed that a bright orange door across the hallway from this room had a sign that said "Playroom."

Sam sat down on an easy chair. He was feeling anything but easy and sat on the edge of the cushion. He had never been in a "home" before. The word seemed distinctly odd in this setting. He had never been in an orphange or a mental institution or any of the places that are not homes but that society, in what he supposed was some weird blend of guilt and do-goodism, decides to call "home."

Was this what Arthur and Janet Hubbell's home was like, he wondered. At that moment a blade of light that lay diagonally across the door was broken. The door swung open and Lucy Swift stood in the frame. An attendant was behind her with one hand on Lucy's elbow and the other on the doorknob. The attendant was a woman. She did not wear a nurse's uniform, but a pink dress with sandals. The lenses in her sunglasses matched her dress.

"Lucy," the woman spoke softly, "we have a friend here. I believe his name is Sam." "We," Sam thought. Where did she get this "we" stuff. He'd never laid eyes on the woman before this moment. "Lucy," she continued in a slow, even-paced voice, "we're in the lounge now. Susan is right here holding your arm. You know what we're going to do?" She did not wait for any answers. "We're going to walk around the room and touch all the walls. I shall place your hands on the wall." The woman turned to Sam and spoke more quickly now. "Lucy often has trouble knowing where the boundaries of spaces are. We find it helps her, she seems more relaxed, if we do this. She's been known to walk right into a wall." The woman opened her eyes wide behind the pink lenses. They were pale eyes with dark irises and reminded Sam of those delicate little flowers with a few precise petals that star the ground in early spring. "You better believe that most of this new wing with all the glass is terrible for someone like Lucy. A lot of the children find it terribly disorienting. But it's worse for Lucy."

She chatted on as she led Lucy around the room, placing her hands on the walls. "Now, Lucy, we're going to take you over here by Sam and sit you down in this pretty bright blue chair near his. Here we are. Now sit, Lucy." She tapped lightly behind Lucy's knees with her hand and pressed down on Lucy's shoulder. Lucy sat. "Good girl." She turned to Sam. "Now, can I get you a Coke or something, Sam?"

"No. No, thanks." He was looking at Lucy in the chair across from his own. There was a coffee table between them. Lucy was looking toward Sam and right through him.

"Well," said the attendant, "I think I'll leave you two. I'll be right next door, Sam, if you need anything. My name's Susan—Susan McGrath. I'll check in on you in a few minutes. All right?"

"All right," Sam said, still looking at Lucy. "I'll be okay." He was not sure, however. He had never been more unsure of anything in his life.

At first he had felt as if Lucy were looking through him. This was still true in a sense, but now there was a slight feeling of panic; for as Lucy continued to look through Sam, he in turn came to feel less real, less solid. It was as if he were appearing to her as a stage prop made of plasterboard, lifeless, without dimension. Even the coffee table between them, sprayed with sunlight, seemed to float, its four legs mere symbols or gestures of function rather than function itself. It was a most peculiar sensation. In this room slashed with light, Sam felt as though reality and its construction were slowly breaking up. Things—real things—were losing their meanings, maybe even their names.

"Lucy!" Sam blurted out. "I'm Sam. Sam Brooks." As soon as he heard his own voice he was fine. He began to talk. "I met you in the woods the other day." She did not blink or move in any way. It was all right. Sam kept talking and as he talked he studied her. The more he studied her, the more Sam realized that Lucy Swift existed within a transparent envelope of unreality—or perhaps it was just a different reality. When he had first seen her that day at the Quabbin, he remembered now, he had thought of her as seeming to be wrapped in some kind of translucent veil that separated her from sound and touch and this world and this reality. Now he knew it was a fact.

It was a shame, Sam thought, that he had decided to sit here. The table between them was bare. He wondered if he dared move her over to the card table where the checkers set lay open alongside what looked like an issue of *National Geographic*.

"Lucy, want to move to the table over there?" Sam asked suddenly, and stood up. His body cast a deep shadow over her. Instantly he had an inspiration. He would move her to the table not by touching her or guiding her with his hand on her elbow as the attendant had done, but by blocking the light with his body. "Lucy, can you get up?" He was facing the brightest part of the light now and talked to her over his shoulder. She did not move. "Wait a minute. I've got an idea." He could turn around and walk backward the twelve or fifteen feet to the table. That way he could face her and talk her along, and his shadow would be cast between them for her to walk in. "You can get up." He'd cheat a little and lift her elbow a bit. She rose instantly. "Now look," he said, dropping his hand away. "We're going over there," he said, pointing toward the table. "Walk on the shadow."

She began to walk. She looked down at his shadow. Then her own shadow spread into the sharp triangle of light on the carpet. She was keeping up with him. The table was farther than he thought, but it was all right. Her shadow now touched his. By the time they were to the second triangle her shadow spread into his and together they blotted out all but a few scraps of light at its edges. They walked within each other's shadows and at last made it to the card table.

Sam commanded Lucy to sit by touching her shoulder and the back of her knees as Susan McGrath had done. Once seated he had high hopes. A *National Geographic* lay open on the table. He glanced at the articles. There was one called "The Preposterous Puffer" that sounded light and fun. Sam started to read the first paragraph. " 'The boot, with its tiny steel tongue, flashed out. Bond felt a sharp pain in his right calf. . . . Numbness was creeping up Bond's body. . . . Breathing became difficult. . . .' " "Holy Toledo," whispered Sam. This was hardly light, nor was it the usual cut-and-dried, hale-and-hearty *Geographic* style he was used to reading. " 'Bond pivoted slowly on his heel and crashed headlong to the wine red floor.' So ends," the article continued, "Ian Fleming's spy novel *From Russia With Love*. . . . In *Doctor No* it is revealed that he (Bond) had been dealt a near fatal dose of fugu poison. . . . It comes from the sex organs of a Japanese globefish, or puffer, a neurologist tells Bond's boss."

The article went on to describe the sometimes deadly but delectable puffer fish that many Japanese people love to eat. This was not an article to read aloud to Lucy, but maybe she would like the pictures. The puffer fish was not in the least deadly looking but, instead, as the title suggested, preposterous in its appearance. He slid the magazine to the middle of the table and flipped to a picture of a cooked puffer. He could not resist skimming a few paragraphs. For an article on food, it was fairly exciting. "Strangely I feel no danger," the author wrote, "but with every bite I sense the thrill." Beats Popsicles and ham, Sam thought. He turned the pages slowly. There was a stunning underwater photo of a fully inflated puffer with a scuba diver hovering above. There was a smaller photo of dried puffers that had been turned into lanterns and decked out with little hats. But Lucy was not looking, not seeing. Although from the very first time he had seen her in the woods he had felt that she somehow looked through people and things, he now felt that "through" was not entirely the right word. Her vision was inward. Her focus was a separate reality, a world nonexistent for him, for others. Sam stopped looking at the magazine and watched Lucy. The limpid, jade green eyes flickered.

Deliberately, but without looking, Lucy picked up a checker and began to twirl it on its edge with the thumb and forefinger of her right hand. It was a tight blur of spinning red on the tabletop. Sam looked at the twirling piece, then at Lucy. As she twirled the checker smoothly, almost fiercely, the illusion of transparency disappeared. The blurred revolutions seemed to pull like a tidal current, drawing Lucy deeper within herself, deeper into the other reality that was an absolute denial of whatever existed without. Yet she was, Sam realized, oddly alert and attendant to the strange world within her.

Sam suddenly picked up a checker, a black one, and began to twirl it. He was not nearly as good as Lucy was. He had to concentrate on the piece entirely and not take his eyes from it; but after trying for a minute he had his checker spinning at the same rate as hers. A minute passed, then another. Although he was not looking at Lucy, he felt something different in her presence. There seemed to be a subtle shift. She was still as deeply withdrawn as ever, as far from the world as one could retreat, but there was less tension.

"Lucy, Lucy," Sam began to whisper softly. He still did not look up. Over and over he whispered her name. It became a litany against which the checker spun. Suddenly the soft whir of the red checker began to wind into a sputtering sound and then there was a small *clap, clap* as the double sphere collapsed into a single disk and lay still—a red checker on the board. Sam let his die too. Slowly Lucy extended her hand toward the black checker, picked it up and set it spinning. Sam reached for the red one, this time looking directly into Lucy's eyes.

Just as in the blind, when Lucy's eye in the lens had suddenly blotted out the sky and the forest, now Sam saw nothing except the liquid jade pools. But Sam had become, in the last few weeks, a good walker in the night woods of the Quabbin. He did not need light to see, nor did he need to see to know. He had his bearings. He could sense the way of a path through the densest growth, to where the water met the shore or the sky the land. "Dark marks," he had come to call them in his night hikes into the woods. They were what the night offered instead of landmarks. And if a person was to walk through the nighttime woods, that person must leave off the day and the land and the known for a different order of things, a different reality.

TWELVE

Sam knelt down on the pad by the camera mount and opened the side door of the Bolex. He peered at the innards of the machine, at the array of small wheels and gears. He popped off the old reel and took a fresh roll of Ektachrome Commercial 16mm color film from his backpack. It would be easy for an inexperienced all-thumbs kid like himself to get lost in the mechanical complexities of the situation. He opened the bright yellow carton and put the new reel in place. He was here because an old man that he cared about even more than he had realized was lying in a hospital "buying time"—hooked up with tubing to chemicals with names he didn't know. He clipped off the fresh end of the film with the clipper that was built into the camera.

Teenagers were supposed to think of life in terms of endless stretches of time, right? How come he had managed to get himself half orphaned and hooked up with an old codger who had only three months left? He felt a rim of tears. Get lost in the mechanics of this, you all-thumbs fool, he thought fiercely. In fact he was becoming more adept with the camera. He was not all thumbs. Maybe just two and a half. His hands worked quickly and fairly confidently. This was his fourth trip into the blind since Gus had taken sick. He closed the automatic threading mechanism and pushed the trigger of the camera so the film would begin to feed in. He had this part down pat, he thought, as he saw the celluloid strip loop through the gate. It was time now for some good footage. He had made his mistakes before, luckily on other birds. One had been an eagle, but not the big eagle, the one they were looking for, hoping for, as a nesting candidate.

He took the tab end of the film as it came out the gate and fed it into the slot on the take-up reel. He let it run to see that it was threaded properly before closing the door. Then he let it run some more so that the exposed part of the film would pass through. He had neglected to do this on an initial try and had flared a shot of a peregrine falcon. But now he was ready. He really wanted that shot. The old 300mm lens had been replaced by an 80-to-250mm that had zoom capabilities. He really had the technical act together. Now if he could only get all kinds of good footage of the birds to take over to Gus's house. Oh boy, Sam thought, better than radiation, better than chemotherapy . . . just five hundred measly feet of properly exposed ECO of the big eagle.

It was at least three hours until dawn. Three hours to wait, think, hope. He wondered if Lucy was awake. He had a feeling she was. Susan McGrath had said during his last visit that Lucy slept a lot during the day, probably to escape the bright light in the building. Sam had a feeling that night and early dawn were Lucy's best hours. He had visited her often since the first time, going first to see Gus in the hospital, then slipping across the street to the Belchertown Home. Their visits had settled into a kind of pattern. They would twirl checkers for several minutes; and on bright days they would walk within the dark pools of their shadows, oases in the desert of white light. She never spoke or made a sound, but on his last visit he had caught her looking toward him, intently. He was turned away from her at the time, but he suddenly knew that he was being *seen*. He had turned around very slowly. Although Lucy had looked at him before, it was always as if she were pretending to watch but actually focused on something inward, within herself. This time it had been different. She was looking out at him—at Sam.

There was a stirring in the air outside the blind and overhead. Sam felt a small tremor deep within him. The big eagle was there. He knew it. He pressed his eye against the rubber cup. It was still too dark. The sky was like an old dark cloth, worn and threadbare, too thin to hold the blackness but still too dark to let through the morning. He could just see something dark against the upper air. At first it seemed formless, a moving stain against the graying sky. He tilted the lens up at a sharp angle. He could see it now, but how could he have felt it? It seemed extraordinary that he had actually felt the stir in the air with the bird that high up. Perhaps he had just sensed it the way he had begun to sense things about Lucy.

The half-light had melted briefly into a woolly gray and then seemed to clear and become limpid minutes before the dawn. The bird kept flying as a soft pink light rose like a vapor on the horizon. The flight feathers on the outer edge of its wings were printed boldly now against the pale light of the eggshell sky. Sam had the bird perfectly framed. He pressed the cable release button that fired the camera. With his other hand he guided the lens to follow the flight. The bird soared on the updraft caused by the rising sun's warming the night-cooled earth. The warmer air rose and, like an invisible pillow, supported the bird's flight so that it never had to flap its wings.

The bird had been gliding a quarter mile or more out from the blind and several hundreds of feet up in the air, but now it tightened its circle and began to bank downward and closer to the blind. Sam had been tracking and filming it for several minutes. While he prepared to use the zoom lens on the bird's closing flight, Sam realized suddenly that as focused as he had been on the big eagle, Lucy had never really left his mind. He had been thinking of Lucy as he had felt, sensed, the bird's first stirrings; and he was thinking of her now as he rotated the lens, drawing the bird rapidly into closer focus. Sam refocused on the white head and zoomed again, pulling the image rapidly into close resolution. There was the crown of white feathers and then the golden flashing disk—the eye fierce and intelligent. Sam backed off slightly now with the zoom and within the frame, like some ghostly double exposure emerging from the strange refractions of the Quabbin woods, another image hovered—the face of Lucy Swift.

"No!" he whispered. But the double image remained.

THIRTEEN

It was an unusually bright morning in the Belchertown Home for the Homeless. Although the glare had been cut to some extent by the newly treated glass, anything that was acrylic, and not real glass, could not be treated. Thus in the lounge the bright geometric shapes cut by the plexiglass openings in the ceiling lay hot and still on the carpet. Sam and Lucy had been shadow walking all morning. The game had evolved somewhat. Sam had created new shadows by propping large cushions and small tables on edge. This morning Lucy, for the first time, had actually helped him create a new shadow by balancing a sofa pillow on edge while Sam got a small end table to support it. They did some checker twirling each visit but the amount of time spent in this activity had decreased, especially since the shadow walking had become more complex. Lucy, now more confident in her ability to gravitate toward the shadows of the room, had started to walk independently and was exploring the perimeters of a triangle of light some eight feet away from where Sam was. Sam propped a pole lamp on a stack of magazines at a forty-five-degree angle, thus bisecting a triangle of light.

"The bisector of the angle opposite the base of an isosceles triangle bisects the base and is perpendicular to the base." A proof based on the isosceles-triangle theorem, chapter five of his geometry text. Had this been an equilateral triangle, Sam would have been able to rotate the lamp and illustrate the three axes of symmetry. The width of the shadow cast by the lamp was approximately that of a person's foot. Lucy and he could walk the bisection from the vertex to the base. Living geometry! But just at that moment Sam looked up and saw Lucy stretched out on the floor along the base of the triangle which she had minutes before been circumnavigating on foot.

"Lucy! Are you all right?" Sam jumped over the propped lamp. She lay very still on her left side facing the triangle of light. He knelt down and leaned over her shoulder, expecting to find her face impassive and completely opaque. The fortress look, he had called it to himself, which indicated Lucy's total withdrawal into her own reality—but there was no fortress. Lucy, relaxed and attentive, was quietly peering at her feet and wiggling them a bit as if to line them up at the point where the base of the triangle met with the shortest side in a right angle. She soon got up and walked to the shortest side of the triangle, placing her toes exactly on the same point. She lay down again, this time placing her body along the short side of the triangle of light.

She moved around the triangle, measuring her body

against each side. Sam watched with wonder. There was no lens now, no optical channel through which to view her and distance himself. Yet Lucy was still within her own world, if not within her fortress. He had sensed almost immediately that Lucy was engaged in some reality, common reality, but perhaps in an uncommon way. She seemed to be a tracker of sorts in a shadowed wilderness. But what was she tracking? Not light, really, he thought as he observed her sit down cross-legged just outside the point of the right angle of the triangle of light. She stared hard at this angle for several minutes. Sam watched. He saw her gaze reach out from the vertex, first along one side and then the other. Then both of her eyes swept the hypotenuse.

As Sam sat at the north point of the figure, Lucy sat at the south. Her eyes were scanning the invisible vertical and horizontal axis of the triangle. She stood up again. This time she began to walk directly toward Sam at the north point. He remained perfectly still, yet some part of him began to move with her. She turned sharply, a precise forty-five-degree angle, and walked southwest along the hypotenuse. At the end of the hypotenuse she did a crisp ninety-degree turn and walked a distance equal in length to the shadow of the hypotenuse. "Each side of the square is the length of the hypotenuse." Sam whispered to himself. Another ninety-degree turn and she headed northeast in the shadows, again a distance that was the length of the hypotenuse. She took one final right-angle turn, which brought her back to Sam at the north point. She had walked a perfect square. She was not tracking, Sam realized suddenly; she was proving— proving the Pythagorean theorem: In a right triangle, the square of the hypotenuse is equal to the sum of the squares of the other two sides.

Sam felt something deep within him turn with fear. He could not run now, not as he had from the blind when the double image had hovered in the lens. There was no double image. There was just this single reality. Lucy Swift had just walked a dark square in a shadowed wilderness around a bright triangle and penetrated a harmony of nature.

The time for their visit was almost up. Sam began to pick up the pillows. Lucy came over and gathered up the stack of magazines just as Sam was lifting the lamp. She smiled quickly at him, a soft, wordless smile. As Sam turned to take the lamp back to its corner he saw two faces peering through the small window of the lounge door. Two men had been watching them through the window. What did it mean? They had always been left alone before. Susan McGrath would come after an hour or so and poke her head in. Now, instead, there were these faces pressed against the glass. One man signaled Sam somewhat jauntily with his forefinger in a kind of intimate salute which Sam did not especially like. He walked quickly to the door and opened it.

"Yes?"

"Oh, we don't mean to disturb you, Sam," whispered the one who had waved. "I'm Dr. Joyce. This is Dr. Naylor. We were just observing uh . . . your . . . uh. . . ." He paused. "Your visit with Lucy. Susan McGrath has told us about Lucy's progress with you and we wondered if we might chat a bit with you after your visit."

Sam was perplexed. He had not thought that anyone was particularly interested in Lucy or ever thought of her in terms of progress.

"Well, I guess so. Is it okay with Susan?"

"Yes, yes. I think she'll join us."

Five minutes later, after he had walked Lucy to her room with Susan McGrath, Sam sat down with the three adults. Susan's violet-tinted lenses today matched her purple dress. She had, Sam had realized after the first few visits, special sunglasses with changeable lenses, so that they always matched her clothes.

"Couldn't treat the glass in here—plexiglass, I guess," said Dr. Joyce. He took out a pair of dark glasses from his vest pocket. "Mark, you got yours?" he asked, turning to Dr. Naylor.

"No. Left them at home. I'll just squint." He proceeded to squint until his eyes were mere slits in his rather chubby face. He shaded the slits with his hand.

"Well now, Sam," Dr. Joyce began. "Susan here has been telling me that you've been visiting Lucy regularly— several times a week for the past few weeks." He paused and took a pipe out of his back pocket and began poking at it with a small metal instrument.

"Yes, sir," Sam said quietly. He was suddenly frightened.

"Can you tell us what prompted these visits? How you came to know Lucy?" Sam said nothing. "Sam?"

"Yes?"

"Can you answer me?"

"Umm. I don't know how it started. Just interested, I guess."

"Can you tell us a little more. Why? Do your parents know about these visits?"

Something icy seemed to form in Sam's chest. His mother did not know. He was not sure why, but for some reason he was not ready to tell her yet. "I . . ." He hesitated.

"Yes, Sam?"

These guys were masters of waiting. Susan McGrath leaned forward a bit and adjusted the violet lenses. The other doctor, Dr. Naylor, picked up a magazine, folded it, and held it to his forehead like a visor. It cast a sharp shadow across his face.

"I don't have a father," Sam said, looking up at Dr. Joyce.

"Sorry to hear that."

It was very hard to tell if someone was sorry, Sam thought, when they wore sunglasses; but he doubted that this news was really breaking up Dr. Joyce.

"And I haven't told my mother yet," Sam continued.

"Any particular reason why not?" Dr. Joyce asked with studied casualness. He was now packing his pipe with tobacco. Sam suddenly wished that he smoked a pipe. It wasn't fair. This guy never really had to focus on him. When things got tight there were eight million things he could do with his pipe without being accused of dodging, avoiding, or being sullen, as Sam was quickly becoming. What could a kid like Sam do? Pick his nose? Kids should be allowed to have pipes in situations like this.

"No," Sam said quickly. "No particular reason. Look." He sighed sharply. "I thought you wanted to ask me about Lucy." An edge had crept into Sam's voice.

"Yes! Yes!" The casualness was dropped. Dr. Joyce fumbled for a match. "Well, Susan says that Lucy's progress is quite remarkable—generally less withdrawn, reduction in twiddling."

"Twiddling?" Sam said.

"Twiddling of objects," Susan offered.

"Eating much better," Dr. Joyce continued. "Toileting behavior."

"Toileting behavior?" Sam asked in a stunned voice.

"Yes, many of these children have problems in terms of elimination. Withholding of stools."

"What children? What are you talking about?" Sam asked, his voice swimming with confusion.

The three adults looked cautiously at one another.

Susan McGrath took off her glasses. "Sam, Lucy is what we call autistic. It is a special kind of mental disorder—infantile autism. We don't know the causes; and with Lucy in particular, we know so very little about her—who she is, where she came from. She was picked up by a state trooper about four years ago. It's hard even to speculate as to the origins of her disorder."

Sam's mind was racing. Words, hollow words meant to describe Lucy swirled in a rage of meaningless sound. Autism . . . toileting . . . twiddling. . . . It was as if they were describing another person.

"It is highly unusual," Dr. Joyce said, "for autistic children to break out of the behavior after the age of five, if they have not done so by then, especially if they have not spoken at all. However, Susan, who has been closest to Lucy for the last few years, thinks that Lucy might just possibly be on the verge of speech."

"We feel"—Dr. Naylor spoke for the first time—"because of some slight indications of more social behavior that Lucy might be headed toward a separation of self from nonself. Her interest in blocks, for example."

"Blocks?" Sam asked.

"Building blocks," Dr. Naylor continued. "She had never before played with blocks. Now she does so regularly. Her structures are becoming more complex. All this indicates an inner freedom to explore what's out there—an awareness of the world out there." These people, Sam was thinking, knew absolutely nothing about

Lucy. In his brief friendship with her, he knew her better than all three of them put together. As Dr. Naylor ran on about the significance of Lucy's tower with the enclosing wall, Sam remembered the square in the shadow and Lucy's remarkable proof just minutes before of the Pythagorean theorem. "In a process somewhat parallel with block play," Dr. Naylor intoned, "Lucy has been able to assume a more normal behavior in reference to elimination. The withholding of stools has almost vanished, less anxiety in terms of—"

"Mark!" Susan interrupted. She put her glasses back on. "You're giving a very Bettelheimish-Freudian interpretation to all this. Let's remember that Sam knows Lucy as a friend, not a case."

"Yes! Yes! Of course!" Dr. Naylor said.

Sam silently thanked Susan but he did not really want to hear any more. He stood up, thinking it was the most polite way he could end the meeting. "Yeah. She's my friend."

Susan grasped Sam's hand. "As a friend, would you take her out, Sam? Just for an afternoon. She never gets out, you know, except with a big group. It would do her a world of good to get out with you and of course an adult—your mom or someone."

Sam looked at Susan. Her eyes were wide and washed with the violet light. "You mean it?" Sam said excitedly.

"I mean it," Susan said, and gave his hand a hard squeeze.

He would take her to the blind. That was easy. The hard part was how to tell his mom. She wouldn't be angry, but he felt awkward about it. How would he explain Lucy, his visits—the whole thing? Since his father had died, he and his mom had been so close. They had shared everything. Now he had held something back. But the real problem was that words were inadequate to describe Lucy and words were his mother's thing. After all, she was an English teacher. But those words that the doctors used were as hollow and meaningless as any he had ever heard.

FOURTEEN

"My recommendation, Philippa, is that you put some of this life-insurance money of Dave's into commercial paper and tax-free municipal bonds for Sam. Oh, Sam!" Uncle Albert looked up. He was sitting at the kitchen table with his mother. Papers covered the entire surface. "Just giving some unsolicited financial advice to your mom. How ya doing, son?"

"Fine."

"Also came by to see if you'd be interested in joining me for some fishing up around North Conway tomorrow."

"Oh, thanks Uncle Albert, but I've got plans."

"Plans?" his mother said, opening her eyes wide.

"Yes, plans!" Sam responded looking directly at his mom and opening his eyes equally wide. Should he drop his little bombshell here? If Uncle Albert had been shocked by his rat shooting, what would he think if Sam suddenly announced his plans for tomorrow? Well, you see, I've got plans with this girl. She's a little nutso. Doesn't talk. Been at the Belchertown Home for the Homeless for the last four years. She was picked up by a state trooper. Found her wandering around somewhere. Sam decided against it. Instead he poured himself a glass of milk, not because he really wanted it, but because he felt that it would make him look like a nice, normal, teenage boy to Uncle Albert. He knew Uncle Albert thought he was weird and for the sake of his mother he thought he should try to improve his image among his relatives. It worked. Uncle Albert clapped him on the back.

"Growing boy, Philippa! Eats you out of house and home, I bet!"

"Yes." Philippa smiled. "He's been lifting weights, too."

"Small ones," Sam added.

"And running." Philippa said.

"Just a couple of miles, Mom." This was getting a bit too much.

"You'll be set for the Boston Marathon before you know it," Uncle Albert offered.

"Oh, no, not me." Sam smiled and took a swallow of the milk.

"Whyyyyy"—Uncle Albert dragged out the "why," then boomed—"not!"

"I hate competitive sports."

"You hate competive sports!" Uncle Albert looked truly shocked.

Sam knew exactly what was coming next. He would have bet his life that "red-blooded" something would be referred to. "What kind of a red-blooded American boy"—Uncle Albert's voice swelled—"from the Midwest, heart of the country, home of the Big Ten universities, hates competitive sports?"

Sam felt terrible, for his mother's sake mostly. He shouldn't have said it. Something about Uncle Albert brought out the worst in him. Thirty seconds ago his mom and Uncle Albert had been standing there like a cheering section for him. *He lifts weights! Rah! Rah! He runs! Rah! Rah! He's friends with an autistic orphan with elimination problems!* "Competition, my boy, that is the cornerstone of our democracy—competition and free enterprise."

"Well." Philippa spoke. "I think Sam is competitive, all right. He's just not keen on team sports."

"Yeah," said Sam quickly. His mother was really something. He would sand and scrape paint for her for the next forty years. "That's it, really. I like to compete against myself. Improve my time, you know."

"Well, that's good!" Uncle Albert looked terrible relieved. "How fast do you do a mile?"

"Oh, I don't know—eight or nine minutes."

"Try to get it down to seven."

"Yeah, I will." Little did Uncle Albert know that this morning it had taken him fifteen minutes to do a mile because he was running around with his head flung back trying to follow the flight of a red-shouldered hawk. Sam didn't really see much sense in running fast through nice countryside. "Maybe I can shave a little off my time," Sam lied.

"Well, eat your Wheaties!" Uncle Albert chuckled heartily.

"Hey, did you see that new Wheaties box," Sam said suddenly. "They put a picture of a guy in a wheelchair on it."

"They what!" exclaimed Uncle Albert. "A paraplegic on a box of Wheaties?"

"He's a wheelchair marathoner," Sam said. Why? Why had he brought it up? What was it about him and Uncle Albert? They were eternally on a collision course. And yes, Uncle Albert, a punk-rock group has replaced the Supreme Court. Ah, what's the world coming to? Sam prepared now to make his last small sally toward a projection of normality. "Well, got to go upstairs and study. Finals next week."

Ten minutes later there was a knock on Sam's door. "Yeah, come in."

Philippa entered. There was a small, crooked smile on her face. "You lifting weights, shaving a few seconds off your mile, or just eating Wheaties?"

"I'm sorry, Mom. I don't know what it is about me and Uncle Albert."

"It's okay. He's kind of a stuffed shirt. I couldn't believe his reaction to the Wheaties thing." She sat down on the edge of his bed and looked over at Sam, who was sitting at his desk with a compass and protractor.

"Was that true?" she asked.

"What true?"

"About the Wheaties box."

"Of course it's true. I wouldn't just make that up for Uncle Albert's discomfort. I think it's great. I don't know why he got so shook. Speaking of which . . ." Sam paused, not knowing quite how to proceed but sensing an opportunity was at hand.

"Speaking of what?" Philippa leaned forward attentively.

"I don't know quite how to say this." Sam pressed the sharp compass tip into the pad of paper and twirled it.

Twiddling behavior! "Speaking of paraplegics and, as they say in school, 'special needs students' . . ."

"Yes?" Philippa said.

"Well, I've met someone with very special needs and I'd like . . ."

Sam and his mother talked into the afternoon. The soft light of the late sun washed across the pine floors and filled the plain room with honey light. They talked about words and language and nonlanguage. Sam told his mother how the doctors had talked about Lucy. The strange words like "autism" and "behaviors" and "patterns." "Those words"—Sam's voice was almost a whisper—"they aren't real. I mean . . ."

"Well, they're just labels," Philippa said softly.

"But they just hang these labels on her for their own sake. The labels aren't really a part of Lucy any more than . . ." Sam searched for a comparison. "Do you remember," he said suddenly, "the year Gram decided not to get a Christmas tree, Mom?"

"Yes. Whatever made you think of that?"

"Remember what Gram said about that pine growing on her lawn outside the living-room window?"

"Yes. She said it was so pretty she didn't need one inside."

"No!" Sam said. "Not exactly. Remember, it had been snowing real hard. And then we got those clear starry nights and we were over there for supper and sitting in the living room afterward, just staring at that twenty-five-foot pine glistening with snow and starlight. Gram turned to Grandpa and said, 'Carl'—I can just hear her—'Carl, we don't need a Christmas tree this year. There's no reason to go and cut down some living thing and hang a bunch of silly balls and lights and tinsel on it. It's as bad as putting lipstick on a baby and has no more to do with Christmas than the Easter bunny has to do with the Resurrection. Look what we've got outside our very own window!' Remember that, Mom?"

Philippa sat very still. Her wide gray eyes looked distant and sad. "I do. I do," she whispered, "and I remember Dad's saying, 'Couldn't ask for any prettier lights than Orion's belt in a clear Indiana sky.' And we all went outside."

"Well, Mom, that's what Lucy's like. She doesn't need words and she doesn't need language, and those labels have nothing more to do with her than tinsel has to do with Christmas or the Easter bunny with Jesus Christ. She's like that tree back in Kokomo on that December night—that pine against the starry black sky. That's Lucy."

FIFTEEN

The next night, just after Sam and his mom had finished their dinner, the phone rang. It was Gus. He was out of the hospital three days early, "fit as a fiddle," ready to go to the blind and check out the repairs that were being made on the hacking tower in anticipation of the new eaglets that would be arriving in a matter of weeks. Night hikes were out for at least two weeks, he told Sam, but he was up for going in tomorrow morning for a few hours. With no snow, the hike would take one-third the time. Sam had been hesitant to say anything to Gus about Lucy, but five minutes after hanging up, he called Gus back and explained about her—the visits and the outing he was now permitted to take her on with an adult.

When Sam and his mother drove up to Gus's house the next morning, he was waiting for them on the steps, thinner and paler, but smiling broadly. "Here I am!" he called out. "One functioning adult for your accompaniment." He climbed into the car. "I hope I can pass muster with the Belchertown folks."

"Don't worry," Sam said. "Half of them don't know what they're doing anyway."

Forty-five minutes later Lucy sat with Sam in the back seat as Philippa drove them to gate eleven. Lucy's silence did not inhibit Gus in the least. He spoke animatedly about the footage that Sam had shot over the past few weeks. Occasionally he would even address a remark to Lucy. It did not seem to matter to Gus that she never answered. Sam could tell that Gus never doubted that Lucy understood his meaning. Any concern or awkwardness that Sam had felt about this outing soon disappeared.

They pulled up at gate eleven and got out.

"Okay," Philippa said, "I'll be back for you in exactly three hours. Don't overdo it. And look, folks," she said, handing them a picnic basket, "there's two sandwiches apiece—ham, tuna, and roast beef—cut into halves. So that means you can mix and match. There's an infinity of possible combinations. Now take it easy. Okay?"

They walked in a line, first Gus, then Lucy, and finally Sam. As soon as Lucy was on the path Sam noticed the change in her movement. It was free and fluid, just as it had been the first time he had seen her almost six weeks before when she had glided into the focus of the camera and hovered like a winged creature in the lens. The wild grace seemed again to possess her body as she moved through the dappled light of the Quabbin woods. They passed the point where ordinarily they would have turned off for the blind and, instead, followed a path leading toward a peninsula of land jutting into the reservoir. It was on the shore of this peninsula that the hacking tower stood.

"Ever see a hacking tower, Lucy?" Gus asked, pointing at the structure. "Hacking's an old falconry technique for raising a young eagle," Gus continued; "well, one old enough to know it's an eagle, but not old enough to know where home is or to have imprinted on a particular spot. The young eagle is caught and placed in a cage in a tree or up on a platform. It's then fed by concealed human beings, so it won't imprint on people instead of on its own species. When it's old enough to fly, the bird is released. We hope then that the birds will imprint on the surrounding countryside and later return to nest and breed."

Sam was watching Lucy. Although she was looking straight up at the tower he could tell that she was hearing Gus. "Our job is to convince some young eagles to call the Quabbin home," Gus continued, putting his hand lightly on her shoulder. "Now Sam," he said, "do me a favor would you and climb up there with your young limbs. See if those graduate students have been making the repairs I ordered when I was in the hospital. You see, Lucy, in about three weeks we're going to have four young eagles arriving by way of Manitoba." Sam had started to climb the ladder, and Gus called out. "Check on the one-way glass, Sam. Make sure both compartments have it and there are cloth screens over the feed-drop doors. Also, if you can climb out on the water side, check the understruts and the bars on the open, exposed side of the cages."

Sam crawled into the space that separated the two cages of the tower. The glass had been installed on either side, and an observer would be able to crouch in the narrow space in between and quietly watch the behavior of the birds. Each cage was about eight feet square and five and one-half feet in height. A perch had been placed diagonally across each cage. The back and one outer side of each cage were solid wall, but the remaining side of each cage had narrow vertical bars. These sides looked out on the reservoir. This was the view, the only view, the eagles would have for five or six weeks. It faced east. The sun would rise with vertical iron bars against it, Sam thought as he peered through the one-way glass. At the moment a cloud hung directly over the island that had once been a mountain and now broke through the still waters of the reservoir. Was that Mount Pomeroy, Sam wondered. In his random reading at the historical society he had encountered many references to children playing and picnicking on Mount Pom, as it had been known. Now it rose out of the water, so still and removed it was hard to believe a human foot had ever touched its earth. Like a fine Japanese brush painting, the island mountain seemed to possess a mystical tranquility.

As Sam crawled out on the narrow ledge to look at the struts, the island mountain loomed larger. The cloud that had floated lazily over it had been brushed away, and now another, long and fleecy, wrapped its tendrils just below the island crown. As Sam sat with his legs dangling over the edge of the platform, the island mountain appeared weightless and oddly unreal, like those cloud-shrouded oriental landscapes painted on scrolls, an ink-wash mountain set against a silken sky.

"How are the struts?" Gus's voice broke his reverie.

"They look okay to me."

"And are pull lines there for the release doors?"

"Let me check." Sam crawled over to one corner. Looped neatly over a cleat were several yards of rope that would pull open the barred doors on release day. Instantly a world that until that day had been viewed through bars would be open to and ready for the eagles, who with their newly fledged flight feathers would see more of this earth than most living things.

When Sam came down again, Gus was explaining to Lucy that there was no chance of seeing eagles today. "When Sam and I want to see an eagle, Lucy, we have to hike in at night to the blind. Less chance of them seeing us that way. But we might as well go over there after lunch. Been so long I kind of miss it. All right with you, Sam?"

"Yeah, but let's eat first."

Sam had spread out the lunch on a flat rock near the water. Lucy was sitting with her back to the reservoir and eating a ham sandwich. She didn't seem to care much whether it was ham, tuna, or roast beef. When Sam had asked her she had merely taken one without looking. As she finished her second half she turned around and looked out at the water, toward Mount Pomeroy. Sam noticed that Lucy was not simply staring at the island mountain in her usual disengaged manner, but seemed to be really scrutinizing it, scanning its contours and gentle slopes for finer details. Sam studied Lucy's eyes. He could tell that what they saw was not just real, but known. Lucy knew what she was looking for.

And Sam observed something else. Between the quick, sure movements of the cognizant eyes was a dimmer light, and cast within this dimmer light was the shadow of another reality. Lucy's eyes swept down suddenly from the island's peak. Slowly, she dipped her hand into the water. Sam looked down too. The reflections of the large cumulus clouds floated on the black water that was now rippled by Lucy's hand. He felt Lucy move slightly. She was on her knees at the edge of the rock, bending over the water. Her thick black curls hung down on either side of her face. The mass of hair was now mirrored by the water and obscured the reflected clouds. The surface was still rippling, and Sam let out a small, low cry as he stared into the water and glimpsed the terror-streaked face reflected on the black surface. Through the curtain of thick hair only an eye and part of the cheek were visible. But there was a rippled image of unforgettable pain and horror.

Lucy's body seemed locked, but with Gus's help Sam moved her away from the water. Within less than a minute she seemed completely recovered, her body supple and moving with a sprightly grace through the woods as she followed Gus with Sam alongside toward the blind. They crawled in. Lucy looked around and settled comfortably on a cushion near the camera platform.

"I left the cake Mom put in back at the . . ." Sam hesitated. "Reservoir," he finally said. He did not want to say the word *water*, it had become so involved for him with the rippling image of the terror-gripped face. "But I think I left some cookies in this tin." He reached for a box by the pallet where he sat, but froze when he saw Lucy's face. He motioned to Gus. Lucy's head was craned upward in the low-ceilinged blind as if she were listening, attuned to something else beyond.

"There's an eagle out there!" Gus's voice was saturated with disbelief. "I know it! I hear it!" And Sam then heard it too. An eagle or a sailplane landing, he thought, for the air now stirred with strong drafts of wind—not just the blown wind of weather, but the pumped, sculpted wind that comes off the wing of a flying creature or contrivance that is landing.

Gus scrambled toward the camera. The rubber eyecup crushed against his face.

"Holy . . . !" Gus's voice stopped. Sam could see him swallow and begin to twirl the knob that shortened the focal length. "The bird's so close I can hardly focus, Sam! Get over and take a look."

Sam crawled over to the still camera. It was mostly used for shooting nonflying, closer-to-earth-type wildlife such as deer. It had a wider-angle lens on it, which was more suitable for viewing something so close. The eagle had landed within ten feet of the blind—an absolutely unprecedented proximity, as far as Sam knew.

"This is weird," whispered Sam.

"Weird? I've never seen anything like this in my life," Gus said. "We came in here in broad daylight. There's no deer meat out there. No food. And yet it lands."

"And it's the big one."

"I know."

"What does it want?"

"It seems almost as if it's waiting for something."

"Come over here, Lucy," Sam said, turning from the camera. Lucy understood and crawled to where Sam was. He moved back. "Now put your eye right up to here," he said, pointing toward the viewfinder. "Here—turn this." He put her right hand on the focus ring. "To the right, toward me a little. If the eagle moves closer it will sharpen the focus."

Within seconds after Lucy had begun to look through the viewfinder, they could hear the bird approaching. They could hear the small pantlike breaths and the clawing of the talons on the hard earth. Gus had pulled the Bolex movie camera out of the opening, and he and Sam sat off at an angle now where they could both have a clear view of the immense eagle as it moved directly toward the other opening where the still camera was mounted. Sam could feel a change in Lucy. He did not need to look at her. It was not just her body, tense now, or her face thrust forward against the camera; her entire being seem attuned to the eagle outside. There was something else profoundly disturbing to Sam. His fingers dug into his palms as he watched her. It was as if the aperture of the camera had become a channel, not just for light, but for another kind of energy. It had become a sort of magnetic channel, not a field which might encompass him, but a narrow channel through which some part of Lucy's being was drawn. It seemed to Sam as though time had stopped. The eagle extended its head until it was almost touching the lens hood and peered straight through the glass optics of the lens at Lucy. Despite her tension, a kind of desperate ecstasy flushed Lucy's face and curled her mouth into the strangest smile.

For a full three minutes the girl and the eagle peered through the optical channel at one another. And Sam sat powerless, as if in a dream with no exits. The eagle then turned and walked away. As the eagle turned, Lucy drew her head back from the camera. She turned toward Sam and blinked. Or he thought she blinked, but in fact her eye seemed to move quite strangely. Within the space of a blink, that fraction of a second, something had flicked across the jade eye from the side, just as Sam had so often seen the eagle's eye turn bright as the thin membrane flashed across it. There could have been another explanation, of course—light bouncing off the camera lens and back through the viewfinder, perhaps? This might cast a bright sunspot on Lucy's eye. But Gus had seen it too. Sam knew, although they never, not even at the end, mentioned it to one another—the third eyelid.

SIXTEEN

> The nictitating membrane, a semitransparent
> third eyelid, is essentially a lens-shaped window
> of high refractive density. It serves to cleanse
> and protect the avian eye, particularly when
> the bird is flying into facing winds. The mem-
> brane moves from the lower part of the corner
> near the bill upward. The thin membrane, an
> adaptation derived from reptiles . . .

"Reptiles!" Sam whispered, and set down the book on
his desk. He didn't really believe that he had seen a
nictitating membrane flicker across Lucy's eye. It must
have been some sort of prismatic oddity caused by a flash
of sunlight on the camera lens. It had to be. How could
a human being have such a primitive biological structure?
This was another one of the hundreds of times every
week, every day, when Sam really missed his dad. His

father had loved to talk about this sort of question. His great love had been not just biology, but evolutionary biology. Birds in particular had become his focus. He was fascinated with them. The fifty-million-year evolution of birds rather dwarfed in comparison the five or six million for people, and raised all sorts of interesting questions. Sam knew that if one took a good hard evolutionary look at human biology, vestiges of certain primitive structures remained. Wasn't that inner pink corner of the human eye sometimes called a "third eyelid"? But still, for this membrane to show up full-fledged in humans—impossible!

Sam continued reading about eagles' eyes. Too bad, he thought, he hadn't come across all this stuff earlier in the semester. He could have done a nice term paper on it. Instead he had written about the Brownings, Elizabeth Barrett and Robert. He had not even liked their poetry that much. Old Robert had a rather tortuous way with words. "Irks care the crop-full bird? Frets doubt the maw-crammed beast?" It was hard to get enthusiastic over a line like that, and the paper was pretty dull until Sam got to their drug habits—opium. He read on in an old college biology text of his dad's.

> The eye of a bird has reached a state of perfection found in no other animal. In its general pattern of construction the bird's retina is fairly orthodox. The excellence of the avian retina lies in the abundance and distribution of the parts. Not only are the rods and cones more numerous and tightly packed than in other vertebrates . . . just as the sharpness or resolving power of a photograph depends on the number and fineness of the silver grains that compose it, so the resolving power of a retina

depends largely on the number and size of its
sensory cells, especially the cones.

The text went on to explain how in birds the cone cells,
with which eagles were particularly well endowed, connected in a one-to-one manner with the optic-nerve-fiber
cells, thus providing each cone cell with an individual
representation on the brain, unlike in humans. No wonder, Sam thought, eagles could see a postage stamp at
five hundred feet or a mouse at nearly one thousand feet.
To see with the clarity of an eagle must be a mind-boggling
experience. But then again, there was not that much mind
to boggle in an eagle. Or was their big eagle different?
Why else had it behaved as it had that afternoon when
he and Lucy and Gus were in the blind? Just as Sam was
contemplating these questions, there was a soft knock on
his door.

"Yeah?"

"It's me," his mother said. "May I come in?"

"Yep."

The door opened and Philippa came and sat on the
bed. "What are you reading?"

"An old biology text of Dad's."

"Oh, what about?"

"Bird vision."

"Well, that's sort of what I want to talk about."

"Yeah?" Sam was perplexed.

"Are you serious about helping Gus with the eaglets?"

"Of course I am!"

"Well, it's going to conflict with haying."

"I could fly out for a long weekend and not miss
much."

Philippa shook her head and looked at Sam levelly.
"Too expensive, for one thing; and this is a situation

that you can't have both ways. It's not fair to Gram and Grandpa or Gus. Each needs your whole commitment if you're going to do it."

Sam knew she was right. He could get out there for two days, it could rain, and haying would be postponed. Then what? But he still wanted to go. "Don't you think they'll be disappointed?" he asked.

"Well, I'm sure they'll be disappointed. But they can hire somebody else for the haying, and you could go out later in the summer for a couple of weeks and have a good long visit. But this weekend stuff won't work, and I'm sure Gram and Grandpa will be pleased that you've settled in here so nicely."

"I haven't settled in that well!" Sam said quickly.

"Well, you've made some friends."

Yeah, he thought—a dying man and a girl with a third eyelid.

"Okay," he said. "I'll call them tonight and tell them I can't come now."

"That's your decision?"

"That's my decision."

SEVENTEEN

The small floatplane drifted silently out of the sky like a speck in the blue. Sam waited on the east edge of the hacking tower. In a few more seconds, the throb of the plane's engine reached him and he could make out the wings. Then, as it banked around the island of Mount Pom, he could see its pontoons. Gus had called him the night before to report. Four young eaglets approximately seven to nine weeks old had been taken. Fifty-two nests had been surveyed in all, but only four were easily accessible with the right number of eaglets at about the right age. Sam had been waiting since dawn. The previous night he had packed in to the Quabbin with his tent and supplies. For the next six weeks Sam would be living there, a few yards from the hacking tower. He had been appointed by Gus as the official caretaker and observer of the eaglets. It had been approved by the State Division of Fisheries and Wildlife, and he would receive a small stipend, although he would gladly have done it for nothing. His job was to feed the birds by dropping fish through the hole every morning, make daily checks on their general health and then spend several hours observing their behavior.

There were slapping splashes and a roar as the plane landed. Sam could see Gus in the seat beside the pilot, waving enthusiastically.

"Ready?" A voice from the ground just beneath the tower called up.

"Okay. I'm coming down." Sam climbed down the tower and got into the boat with Edward Kimberly, a man from the State Division of Fisheries and Wildlife. They started the small outboard and headed toward the plane. The whir from the propellers ruffled the water for at least one hundred feet around. But as they drew closer, the pilot cut the engines. A small door swung open. Gus leaned out and gave the thumbs-up sign. "We got 'em!" He looked good; exhausted, but his was perhaps as happy a human face as Sam had ever seen.

LIVE BALD EAGLE. The words were stamped boldly on an angle across the tops of the fiberglass cages. Every pulse in Sam's body seemed to be beating wildly as he took the first cage and set it on the floorboards of the boat. He crouched down immediately to look inside. Had he really known what to expect? No, not at all. He realized that as soon as he peered through the heavy mesh. There was nothing babyish about an eaglet. It was the wildest thing he had ever seen. The eyes were keen. The talons were several inches long and able to tear, to kill. By definition the eaglets were immature—their heads still dark and without the crown of white, the wings not fully fledged. Yet already they had attained sixty percent of

118

their body weight and, Sam thought, one hundred percent of their fierce wild spirit.

Within half an hour the four transport cages had been hoisted up to the hacking platform and the eaglets introduced into their new environment, their home for the next five weeks. Two eaglets had been put in each cage on the tower. The space in the cages, which had appeared ample to Sam before, seemed to contract as he watched through the one-way glass and saw the agitated young eaglets flap their wings and move about in the enclosure.

"You going to be all right here, Sam?" Gus asked.

"Sure. Sure."

"Well, I'm bushed. So I'll get on home. You know what to do. The fish are down in the box by the float. We'll keep them on suckers for the first few days. Pound or so a day per bird. You got the behavior charts?"

"Yep, in my tent."

"Got everything you need for yourself?"

"Yep."

"Be sure to put on plenty of that repellent. The mosquitoes are fierce out here this time of year."

"You're sure the eagles won't smell me when I go up to observe?"

"No. Not at all. Birds, remember, especially eagles, don't smell much. Their olfactory nerves are almost nonexistent compared to mammals'. So don't worry. Wear the repellent."

"Okay."

By six o'clock that evening everyone had left and Sam was alone, as alone he guessed as he had ever been in his life. All the forty-seven gates having been closed and locked, he was most likely the only human being in one hundred twenty-six square miles of wilderness. He had at times been uneasy here, but not now, not this night.

He wasn't sad or scared. He was sitting on a spit of rocks just to the south of the hacking tower, watching the water change from black to orange to rose under a setting sun. There had been a time, Sam remembered, back in their old house in Kokomo, when he had been afraid to go upstairs to the bathroom by himself. He had a cousin, Willy Bigelow, who used to think that there were dragons in the toilet, dragons that were like those little flat dry sponges. When you flushed the toilet they would inflate and come to life swollen and full of terror. Willy never flushed a toilet at night. Dragons were Willy's fear.

Sam hadn't really had any like that, but he had never liked the story of Snow White. That had scared him a lot. It wasn't so much the evil stepmother or the dark woods. It was the glass coffin at the end. To Sam that was the scariest illustration in the book. But in general Sam's fears as a child had not been of a specific nature. They weren't dragons or monsters or ghosts or wicked stepmothers but vague terrors that resided in dark corners and wrapped themselves in shadows. The worst fears, he thought, aren't the ones that come with scales and fangs and tongues of fire. The worst fear had been shaken out of the darkness for him on that winter night on Route 465, and it was not scaled and primeval. It was a sixty-year-old Indianapolis banker with a .15-percent level of alcohol in his bloodstream returning from a party. He survived without a scratch, and David Brooks died of a broken neck. So the fear had been defined, and now, in the slowly vanishing light of a summer day, Sam sat in this accidental wilderness without fear or longing or loneliness. He missed his dad, but that was not really loneliness anymore. And he was not sad tonight, not with the still, rose-gold waters and the clouds that stretched low and long like whales streaming through the sky.

Sam climbed the tower once more before turning in. The eagles were calmer. They sat on their perches, looking east through the bars toward Mount Pom. In his tent Sam fixed himself a sandwich, drank a cup of milk and turned in. It was not yet completely dark, but he wanted to be up before dawn. Just before he went to sleep Sam remembered thinking, not whether the eaglets missed their parents, but how they missed them. They must miss them in some vague way, he thought sleepily, but how. What is it that they miss exactly?

By seven the next morning Sam had been sitting crouched with a clipboard in his hand for over an hour. There were several columns across the paper on the board, each one with a different heading: resting, preening, wing stretching, wing flapping, escape behavior, feeding, interaction. Every five minutes Sam would make a check mark under one or more of the categories after observing a bird. So far the resting column had the most marks. Sam guessed that the eaglets weren't so different from human babies in this respect. Eating, sleeping and growing were the first order of business. Two hours earlier he had dropped the fish into each cage.

Staring at the eaglets, Sam thought of Lucy. She too was measured and checked, observed rather than known. Was he so different from the doctors in the home? Was it possible to ever "know" an eagle? Gus had, he was sure. Sam shifted to a more comfortable position. He wondered if the memories of parents were already dimming for the young eaglets in their human-built nest, fed by a concealed provider, namely himself. Was the print of flight fading, the once-steady image of wings against a sky? How in the space of the next few weeks would the eaglets ready themselves for flight? Without coach or guide, without living example, without the steady repetitive image of parent winging home, banking and gliding, taking off and alighting—was it not an awesome proposition, the ultimate dare to grab the wind and break free alone?

EIGHTEEN

Sam was on Lucy's right side, Gus on her left. The three were crouched in the central space of the hacking tower. They had been observing through the one-way glass for less than a minute when the smaller eagle in one of the cages, presumably the male, began moving on its perch closer to the observation wall. It then got down from its perch and came deliberately up to the one-way-glass window through which Lucy had been watching. The eaglet brought its beak right against the glass. It did not peck at the window but remained very still. It could see Lucy, Sam was sure. His heart raced. His mouth was suddenly dry. He reached around to touch Gus, who was observing the other cage. Gus turned. Sam nodded ever so slightly toward Lucy. The old man's eyes opened wide in disbelief. "So much for one-way glass," he mouthed the words.

In almost ten days Sam had never once observed a bird approaching the glass.

Lucy had ceased to look at the eaglet. She was looking east, to the bars and to the island mountain beyond the bars. Her mouth, half opened, seemed tense. Sam could see the small muscles of her throat and neck move. Her lips too moved ever so slightly, as if she was trying to arrange them. She swallowed once and then opened her mouth again. Sam was taut with excitement, expectation.

Now Gus, too, was looking at Lucy. They could both see it. The shape of a word was on her lips, the contour of sound in her throat. She turned quickly toward Sam, her eyes wide and questioning.

No word was ever spoken, but they both knew what Lucy was asking. *Why are the eagles caged?* Sam's excitement grew. For the first time Lucy was responding to a world outside herself. She was clearly perceiving that there was a space around her and that within that space was a place in which living things had been enclosed, cut off with wood and metal bars. She turned and looked at the metal bars again and then back to Sam, recognition in her eyes. It's the bars, Sam thought, so similiar to the bars within the fortress of her own mind. The bars, although recognized, were hardly understood.

"Lucy, the birds will be free soon," Sam whispered. "They're not going to be caged forever." Lucy had brought her face close to Sam's, as if she was not simply listening but almost inhaling every word. "They're too young to fly now. Their flight feathers haven't hardened off yet. Their wings aren't strong enough yet. They have to grow and practice more," Sam said, and then continued eagerly, "but they're getting there. They used to just sit around a lot, but this week they started some serious wing flapping. That's their preflight exercise. When they're ready, Lucy, we'll let them go. I promise."

When the three of them came down the ladder the sun was just setting, sinking fast toward the dark line between water and sky. They stood facing west on the beach of the peninsula, the view blocked to the eagles, and watched the odd optical distortion in the sun's shape as it pressed down through the atmospheric refractions toward the water. The sun glowered a deep orange and became a ragged oval as it met the water. There was a dark speck. Sam blinked. For a split second he thought the speck was actually in his eye, floating across the cornea. But it was not. The speck was in the sky. The sun elongated now, and Sam could just begin to make out the jagged wing edge printed against the sky, burnished by the last flares of a vanishing day.

It soared and rode the updrafts for several minutes. But then it began to beat its wings and pull forward toward shore, to Gus and Sam and Lucy. It was the big eagle. The three of them stood silently as the bird landed just a few feet in front of Lucy.

It was the first time Sam had ever observed a mature bald eagle without lens, window, screen, or any other channel. The three humans and this creature stood close together; yet, as Sam would later reflect, it was the eagle's presence that dominated. Her talons, spread as wide as a large man's hand, seemed to grip the earth. The white feathers of her head tapered into the dark shoulders in much the same manner that a knight's helmet with its chain-mail hood underneath becomes confluent with the armor. Always before when Sam had observed the eagle from the blind she appeared wary, her coat slightly ragged in a kind of bristling reaction that showed her both on her guard and aggressive. But now the eagle was not

wary. Her coat was sleek, the power a glistening suggestion enfolded by the wings at rest, the eyes small dark
spheres of intelligence. Sam knew that no matter what
human leader he should ever encounter, king or queen,
president or general, he would never be in the presence
of a more inherently regal creature.

NINETEEN

"This is not an environmental-impact statement," the man said, waving a sheaf of papers in the air. He was bald and wore half glasses that slipped down his nose. "This is an addendum dreamed up by QUORP."

"I object, Mr. Chairman!" Another man had jumped to his feet from his chair behind the QUORP table in the hearing room.

"Okay, tacked onto the master plan," said the first man, who was a representative from the Massachusetts Audubon Society and a member of the QUAVA board. "Tacked on with hopes that it would pass as an impact study. But it won't! It talks about traffic and access and people and nonpolluting recreational activities—what could be there. But it does not talk about what *is* there— the animals, the winter-feeding population of bald eagles and the possibility in the almost immediate future of a breeding population of bald eagles."

"Possibility—hardly a reality." The man who had objected stood up again and shook his finger. "Breeding eagles are not there now."

"And they won't be, nor will the winter feeders of this endangered species if you have your way!"

"Well, Mr. Dopplemeyer, seeing as you were so specific about clarifying what is not in the Quabbin area as opposed to what is, I thought it only consistent to point out that there is no evidence whatsoever of breeding bald eagles. The Massachusetts Audubon Society has tried to establish them over the years."

"Four years, to be exact," Dopplemeyer interrupted.

"Nonetheless, there is at this moment in time"—the QUORP representative drew out the phrase, weighing each word—"not a single breeding eagle in the Quabbin and let us not get overly emotional about a nonexistent resident when fifty years ago thirty-five hundred residents were summarily evicted." There was a swell of applause and cheers.

Sam stifled a yawn. He knew how the rest of the meeting would go. He had the script down pat. QUORP's ace card was one that Gus termed "retroactive justice." It seemed to work every time. People cheered, brave men cried, etc., etc., Sam thought. The argument went, roughly, that because the original valley dwellers had been so unjustly denied their homes, schools, businesses and way of life, their descendants should be allowed to canoe, ski, hunt and snowmobile across, over and through what had been at one time their parents' and grandparents' homes. It was about as stupid an argument as Sam had ever heard, but it worked wonders. The thing that angered Sam about the whole argument was not just its simplemindedness, but its brazen manipulation of people's emotions.

He thought about the newspaper clippings he had read at the Swift River Valley Historical Society. There was a Mrs. Howe, wife of the postmaster, who, with her husband, had refused to move until the last minute. For months on end she heard the cacophony of the wrecking—the bulldozing, the blasting, the sizzling fires. "I don't think I can stand it," she was quoted in the newspaper as saying about the terrible noise of the destruction. Sleeping or even thinking, she said, was almost impossible. So she knitted all day long. She was old, and stunned by what was happening around her. Another elderly man had said, "Too old to make new friends. It's easier for the young folks, but the oldtimer—just too old! Reckon I'll stay put until they take me away in a rowboat."

Would it have helped either one of these people, Sam thought, to know that their great-grandchildren were swimming in the billions of gallons of water that covered their homes? Would it have cheered their eternal sleep all that much?

Although there were mutterings from various members of QUAVA that the addendum would never stand up in a court battle as an impact statement, Sam was not so sure. So far, QUORP strategies had stood up fairly well, and as far as Sam could tell support for QUAVA was weakening. There were fewer people at the meetings and much less attention given in the newspapers.

Gus and Sam walked to Gus's car after the meeting let out. It was late afternoon. "Mom told me to ask you for dinner. Lucy's going to be there," Sam said as they climbed in the car.

"Sure. Sounds good. Don't eat much these days, you know."

"She'll understand," Sam said.

Gus drove out of the parking lot. For the first few minutes they didn't say anything. Then Gus broke the silence with a chuckle.

"Sure wish that big eagle would give us a hint of her plans." He tried to make the remark sound light, but he was not that convincing. He sighed. "It all depends on her."

"What do you think the chances are that she'll nest here?" Sam asked.

Gus, looking straight ahead at the road, took one hand off the wheel to gesture. He started to speak. His voice cracked slightly. He coughed, began again. "I don't know, Sam. Rationally thinking about it, it seems it should happen. But then again, I keep thinking if she does come back to nest and breed what a piece of great luck and if she doesn't . . . " His voice dwindled off. He swallowed. "Not to mention that it takes two to tango and she's got to find a mate and the mate could just as easily take her off to his place! So maybe you have to say fifty-fifty, depending on which bird has the strongest will."

When they walked around to the back of Sam's house, they found Philippa and Lucy kneeling side by side in the Japanese garden. They were tamping moss into a space formed by three large rocks.

"Hi," Philippa greeted them. "We're just finishing up here. Be done in a minute."

"Don't let us interrupt," Gus said.

Interrupt. Sam wasn't used to "interrupting" his mother. The word jarred him. He could see Lucy's tarnished locket swinging out from her neck as she bent over the moss. Although she appeared oblivious to Sam and Gus's arrival for several minutes, she seemed quite attuned to Philippa and would pause occasionally, inclining her head toward Philippa. One time she even touched Philippa lightly to draw her attention to what she was doing.

Philippa stopped work and got up. "These new rocks really do finish off this corner nicely, don't they?" She didn't wait for an answer. "Lucy just loves working here. See that little hill in the center? That was her idea, to pile up some of the topsoil and make a little moss-covered mound—a mountain, really."

A mountain, exactly! Sam almost gasped as he recognized a replica in miniature of Mount Pom. The contours of Mount Pomeroy were not especially distinctive. But Sam had been observing its peak for almost four weeks from the banks of the reservoir, from up in the tower and through the barred east view as the growinig eagles saw it. Lucy looked straight up at Philippa and then over to Sam and smiled.

She's come so far, Sam thought. She smiles. She touches people's hands and arms for attention. She would talk soon. He was sure. Then why did he feel so odd now, almost sad? And why had Lucy created this miniature landscape—not landscape, world. What did it mean? Until now there had been a world hidden within Lucy. But now that world was beginning to emerge, and Sam found it unnerving, confusing and frightening. His own admission startled him. He was scared, really scared for the first time in eighteen months.

That night Sam almost didn't return to the Quabbin. He was strongly tempted to sleep at home in his own bed. He wanted to hear his mother's rhythmic breathing across the hall or her quiet midnight putterings if the night was a sleepless one for her. Sometimes when she couldn't sleep she would tiptoe into Sam's room and brush a hand over his forehead or trace his jawline lightly with a fingertip. If he was awake he would often pretend to be asleep. It was such a light touch, not intrusive at all, just gentle and caring. No matter what kind of arguments or nagging had gone on during the day he knew he looked fairly decent to her then. This, after all, was when kids were supposed to appear most angelic. Or maybe it wasn't his angelic look that appealed to his mom, maybe it was his ability to sleep. Maybe she was just an insomniac mother admiring and envious of a slumbering child.

"So, do you really want to go back tonight?" Philippa asked after they had dropped Lucy at the home.

"Yeah, I better."

"You could skip one night and get up early tomorrow in time to feed them. I'd drive you over."

"Naw. Only a week more until release day. Then I'll be through. I want to keep a close watch on things for now."

"Okay."

Sam crawled into his sleeping bag and opened the "star flap" on the ceiling of the tent directly over his head. He had cut out a twelve-inch-square flap of canvas earlier in the summer, fit it with a piece of nylon screen and secured Velcro tape around the perimeters of his hole and its flap. He was now mosquito-proof and star-ready, the only requirements for sleeping in a tent on a summer night in an accidental wilderness. He settled back and looked out the square, thinking about release day. Six more days and the eagles would be free. Their wings had fledged out significantly and grown stronger. The primaries were well formed, articulating smoothly with the secondaries. It would be these flight feathers that would generate lift as they struck the air at right angles to the bird's body.

Sam could tell that the birds were getting considerably more lift in the cage, even between the perch and ceiling. Would they be anxious, hesitant, he wondered? On the brink of flight, would there be some sudden incandescence in the brain, an ignition of instinct, a brilliant illumination of the dim pattern of flight and then airborne would they float off into the sky? Sam thought of eagles and watched the Great Bear climb the black dome of the summer night. One by one he picked out the seven stars. It was an unusually clear night. He found Leo quickly and within Leo, Regulus and Denebola. He opened his eyes wider. His breathing became softer. This was a night for scanning. Lyra, Cygnus, he could find them all on a night like this—bright configurations in a swirling universe. A night not just for scanning with eyes, but for reaching out with mind and dreams and imagination.

He had read about a cosmic mystery of immense proportions in the newspaper's science section. What a mystery it was! A major part of the universe had not arranged itself into starry configurations at all, but was in fact missing, according to scientists, an invisible mass that earth's most powerful telescopes could not detect. Like Lucy, Sam thought as he drifted near the horizon of sleep. Beyond the flickering galaxies of her eyes lay undetectable universes.

He did not hear it, but there was a wingbeat just outside the star flap. The central pole of the tent shuddered briefly, but Sam did not feel it. He was fast asleep as the big eagle alighted. The third eyelid remained tranquil, not as it was when she was in flight, beating into facing winds, flicking, adjusting for sudden refractory changes to keep the eye wet and clear. The flight would come, but the night was long and boys who sleep on the edge of a new universe need watching.

TWENTY

The day before release day, Sam and Gus entered the cages for the first time since the eaglets had arrived. There was a great deal of flapping and hopping about, but they efficiently caught each bird, then hooded it in order to calm it for its preflight physical. Dr. Edgeworth Morton, who waited below, examined each eaglet after it was brought carefully down the ladder to him. His main focus, after establishing that the birds were in good health, was to determine whether their feathers had hardened off. He was particularly interested in the tail feathers, to which tiny radio transmitters would be sewn.

"Yes, these are definitely hardened off."

He gently separated the tapered tail feathers of the eaglet that Gus held for him. "See, Sam, while the feathers are still forming they get nourishment from the bird's circulatory system. There's a soft pulp center, originally a dermal papilla, a kind of connective tissue. It contains many, many blood vessels that nourish the growing feathers. When growth is completed the blood vessels dry up. The feathers are disconnected from the bird's circulatory system. Very energy efficient, considering how much it would require to nourish a plumage of thousands of 'living' feathers, were they still connected to the circulatory system." He paused. "Okay." The doctor turned around and took a very small drill out of his bag. "We can now perform a virtually bloodless operation here.'

Within fifteen minutes Dr. Morton had drilled a tiny hole in the shaft of the bird's central tail feather and had completed sewing on the two-and-one-half-ounce radio transmitter with surgical thread. Dr. Morton explained. "The transmitter will allow each bird to be tracked during the first year of freedom. When the bird molts its feathers next year, the transmitter will fall off with the old feather. Its battery will probably be dead by then anyway."

By the end of the morning all four birds had been equipped with identical equipment and declared ready to go. The "go" would be in less than twenty-four hours.

"Lazybones!" A voice shouted down through the star flap. Sam flinched in his sleeping bag.

"What? What?"

"Sun's been up for a full minute and you still sleeping." Sam rolled onto his back and looked out the square. Gus's face, lively and smiling, peered down.

"Today's the day." Sam blinked and sat up.

"And a minute of it gone already!" Gus said.

"You must have got up at the crack of midnight to make it here so early."

"Come on out. Quit grousing. I got a blueberry pie

from Mildred. Got any hot water for coffee?"

"No coffee, just tea."

"Tea's fine. Not one of those weird herbal ones with funny-sounding names, I hope."

"No, just regular."

Sam walked carefully, carrying two mugs of hot tea down to the water's edge just beneath the tower, where Gus crouched on a large, flat, circular rock. He was cutting the pie in half with a Swiss Army knife. "Got some forks?"

"Yep." Sam set down the mugs on the stone. He took two forks out of his back pocket and handed one to Gus. "What was this thing?" he said, looking down on the stone.

"This thing we're sitting on?" Gus took a bite of pie and pointed down with his fork at the stone.

"Yeah."

"Millstone. Royce's gristmill used to be right around here. Several mills in the valley back then. All kinds— woolen, saw, grist."

"Hmmm." Sam took a bite of pie and watched the sun, just above the horizon, turn pink the fleece of some low-streaming dawn clouds. "You came from Enfield, didn't you?"

"Smith's Village."

"That was near?"

"Oh, it was really part of Enfield. Enfield was divided into two villages really, upper and lower. The upper one was called Smith's Village. That's where our house was, but my dad's store was down in the lower village."

"What kind of store did he have?"

"General store. Sold a little bit of everything, you know."

"Did you work there?"

"Sure, all the time. My sister and I loved it down at the store. Before we were old enough to really help, we'd go down there and play behind the counter. Make hide-outs from old packing boxes and empty crates. I remember once, Becky and I, we were trying to hide from my dad, or customers, I don't know which. Guess we wanted to pop out and scare them. Well, we crawled into a carton that some soap had been packed in and I took to having a most terrific sneezing fit. Oh, my, Becky was mad." Gus paused. "You know that's got to be one of my very first memories. I couldn't have been much more than three at the time."

"Was Becky older?"

"Yep. She must have been six or so. Pretty as anything. She was the Statue of Liberty for our Fourth of July parade."

"Statue of Liberty? How do you do that?"

"Well, she wore a kind of drapy-looking thing with a crown and held a torch. She wanted to paint herself silver, but my mother wouldn't hear of it."

"What were you?"

"Let me see. I think I was an Indian. Yep. Me and Bill Rice and another kid built a wigwam float and painted ourselves up like Indians. I think there was a big battle over which one of us would be Chief Many Waters."

"Chief Many Waters?" Sam asked.

"Yep. Quabbin—in Nipmuc the word means Many Waters. That was the name of the old chief."

"You're kidding!" Sam said.

"No, I'm not. Reservoir got its name from the Indians, branch of the Nipmucs. Lived in the valley when the first white folks came. One of the sachems, chiefs, was supposedly called Nani Quabbin. 'Nani' is another word for chief. Chief Quabbin."

Sam stopped eating to consider this. "Kind of weird, don't you think, considering we're sitting here eating blueberry pie and overlooking all this water? Many waters—kind of like a destiny fulfilled, or something."

Gus didn't say anything for a minute. He just looked out across the water. "Destiny? I'm not sure. I'm not even sure what the word means anymore. It's hard to talk of destiny in a nuclear age. But it was hard then too." He was quiet for a while. "If you think that's odd, the name Quabbin, how about this for a strange coincidence. The man most responsible for the creation of the reservoir, its chief proponent and major engineer, was a certain X. H. Goodnough. Xanthus Henry Goodnough. Mr. Goodnough also shared the name Xanthus with a certain river god in the Iliad who tried to overflow the banks of his river in an attempt to drown Achilles. Another Xanthus from classical times was a historian, a Lydian. Among his writings was one describing a drought during the reign of Artaxerxes. Our own Mr. X. H. Goodnough had a bit in common with both these fellows. He described with great persuasion a water shortage and impending drought for Boston, if certain river gods were not unleashed, diverted and ultimately impounded in a reservoir."

"That's amazing!"

"A little bit of destiny at work, or at least at some name play."

Sam scooped another bite of pie onto his fork. "I'm glad my parents just called me Sam." He looked out at the water and Mount Pom breaking through the surface. Things were so easy when it was black and white, right or wrong, but this accidental wilderness raised some complicated questions. So much had been destroyed, but out of that destruction a new, unexpected world had been created. At this moment it did not seem necessary to question any of it. On a clear morning like this, to sit in the wilderness on a round, flat stone and eat blueberry pie with an old man, that seemed right and good. In fact, nothing had ever tasted so good to Sam in his life. Once, years before, he and his cousin Willy had gone to the state fair. Their grandfather had given them money for ice cream and let them ride the Ferris wheel all by themselves for the first time. They had held their cones in their outside hands and their inside hands had become ten interlocking fingers grasping the safety bar together. Sam always remembered the taste of that ice cream as he and Willy licked their cones and rode together high into the August night in the ring of bright lights. But this was better. This blueberry pie tasted better than anything. It was the best.

Lucy arrived with Philippa shortly before eight that morning. There were two or three people from the State Division of Fisheries and Wildlife as well as some graduate students in biology from the university. Sam and Lucy and Philippa took up watch on a rock with a good view about fifty yards from the tower, where a screen of pines gave them good coverage, so as not to distract or disturb the eagles. Gus with a motion camera was in a small boat, a half mile offshore. Dr. Morton would pull the ropes that would swing open the bars of the cage. Sam could see Dr. Morton loosening the ropes. In another few seconds the doors would swing open.

It was a hot, windless morning. The doors squeaked. The cage was open. There was not a sound. Nothing came out. Sam had been standing with his palm against a tree. He pressed it hard against the bark. Nothing was happening. Then, from the cage nearest to him, Sam saw an eagle's head dip out and look down. *Don't look down!* Sam thought, silently coaching the bird. *You'll never do it. Look out! Look at the sky. That's your country.* He could feel rivulets of perspiration running down his cheeks and throat.

Tentatively the eagle walked out on a horizontal strut to the very end. It spread its wings. Sam's breath locked in his throat. Then, just as suddenly, the bird folded its wings tightly against its body and looked down. *No! No! Not down, up! Up! Birdbrain! Oh, rats, I didn't mean it. Sorry. Where is your birdbrain?* Had the image dimmed beyond recall, Sam wondered, the print faded by weeks without parents? *Orphan bird! Bleach-brained orphan bird!* Maybe they had taken them too young, before the image had printed. Maybe they did not know they were eagles. Maybe they thought they were cows or beavers. Sam was so close to hysteria that he never did remember actually seeing the eagle begin to spread its wings. But suddenly there it was—seven feet of wingspan. There was an effortless stroke and the bird lifted off the platform. Immediately two other eagles flew directly out of the cages. The fourth eagle took three hops to the end of the strut and, without ever looking down, spread its wings and joined the others, who were now soaring and gliding on the warm air currents. Sam could feel his mother's hand gripping his shoulder and Lucy ever so lightly touching his elbow. He tracked the birds with high-powered binoculars. If Eskimos had twenty different words for snow, Sam thought, then eagles, if they could speak, would have twice as many for wind and air. With their wings in the air they were like sculptors. He could see the long, tapered primaries which, in their unique arrangement, could spread like fingers and make innumerable minute adjustments. These primaries, each one like a wing in itself, chiseled the wind, the air, the billowed drafts and made the eagle with its magnificent powers the champion of flight.

His mother had released her grip on his shoulder, but he felt once more Lucy's touch on his elbow. It was not just a light touch now, but more of a tapping. He lowered the binoculars. There was a wet streak down the middle of each of Lucy's cheeks. She turned to Sam and in a very low, rich voice spoke two words: "Home . . . free."

11 THE LOST VALLEY

TWENTY-ONE

"Lucy talking pretty good now, Sam?" Gus settled back on the pallet. He had just regained his breath and voice following a chest-quaking coughing fit.

Sam was uneasy. He didn't feel that Gus should be spending nights out in the blind. Although they were barely past the middle of August, the evenings had turned cool. There was a trace of fall in the air.

"Yeah. Mostly with me. Not much with the hospital people. She talks with my mom some." It had been just a week since the eagles' release and Lucy's first words. Since then her progress had been amazing. It was not as if she were a baby beginning with single words and then advancing to two-word phrases and gradually building real sentences. She did not really have to learn the language. She seemed to have all the vocabulary and structures of speech. She merely had to accustom herself to the fact that these were now all available to her for use. When the eagles had been released, something within Lucy had been released too; and something in Gus had also changed since that day.

For Sam this latter change was profoundly disturbing. Gus had seemed so happy, so completely joyful and euphoric on that day when the four eagles had flown out of the tower. He was still happy, but Sam could tell that he was weakening. It was as if he were wasting away before Sam's eyes. He still went to his doctor, and there had been no radical change detected in his condition. He claimed he had not lost weight, but his face seemed to have caved in.

The light in the kerosene lamp grew dimmer. A curve of forehead, a suggestion of a jaw, a shadow cast by a brow bone could barely be deciphered. The known physiognomy, the facial topography, was disappearing like landmarks in a fog, and yet in Sam's mind the face grew clear. Then the lamp flickered out and Sam looked toward Gus through the darkness.

"Gus . . .?"

"Yes?"

Before he spoke Sam knew his voice would have that tinny cheerfulness that he hated. But he had to say something, anything, to shore up the old man and his hopes that the eagles would someday return. But what could Sam say?

"I'll never forget how that third eagle looked coming off the platform. He must be the star flyer of the group."

"Huh." Sam wasn't sure if the noise that came from Gus was a laugh or not. "The Chuck Yeager of eagles."

"Who's Chuck Yeager?"

"Old-time test pilot, best ever." Gus paused. "Does TV commercials now."

"When did he fly?"

"World War II through the early fifties."

Sam was quiet for a moment. "Back in the thirties, how did it happen—the reservoir and all?" he asked suddenly.

There was a soft sigh in the darkness. "Oh, it didn't just 'happen,' like one quantum leap from valley to ocean. It happened in little pieces over long stretches of time. Rumors had been swirling around as early as the First World War." He paused. "It's a long story, though. You know, like all things complicated—people, towns, nations, hard to know where to begin a story, a history, to do it justice. Where do you start? When the first bulldozers rolled in, the dynamiting first took place? Or do you go back eons to when the first glaciers gouged out the valley? Complicated business, beginnings and endings of things."

"Well," Sam cast around for a way to keep Gus talking, "what were the people like who used to live here?"

Gus laughed a low chuckle in the night. "A lot of them were farmers. Farming here, well, you had to be a little crazy to farm in New England. Not like Indiana, I guess. Rock farming, we call it here—a lifelong, deep involvement with rocks. So if you wanted to farm, your first harvest was rocks. This whole valley was laced with stone walls built from the rocks taken out of the soil where people wanted to farm. It wasn't really farmland at all in the proper sense. Any fool knew that. But the land had a loveliness to it. Nice contours, you know. Stands of big shady trees. Gentle hills—so green! And then there were these low stone walls, hand built, following every contour of the land.

"Houses were nice too. If you were farm folk, you most likely had a typical clapboard farmhouse, the kind that tends to ramble a bit. You started with just the basics in terms of space—kitchen, bedrooms, parlor, buttery. Then as the family grew, as the animals multiplied, you kept pushing out from the kitchen. Twenty, thirty years you're out maybe one hundred feet and are connected with your barn. Nice in the wintertime. If you weren't a farmer and lived down in the villages, well, those houses didn't ramble. Not one bit. They stood their ground like straitlaced Victorian ladies sniffing the air, a few of them, with their fancy cupolas and such. Our house had a nice porch that wrapped around the west side. It had been in the family forever." Gus paused. "Forever being 1795. That's when my family came up from Connecticut. Jediah Early had got the land which had been granted to veterans of the Narragansett Indian Wars."

"He farmed the land?" Sam prompted, totally absorbed.

"Nope, he didn't come to farm. Jediah had tried that down in Connecticut. He had his mind set on other kinds of energy. He was set on building a mill. Two branches of the Swift River flowed right through the village. That meant excellent waterpower; and there was no mill there at that time. So folks could till rocks if they wanted, but Jed borrowed three hundred dollars from his father-in-law and started a sawmill. Actually the first mill was on a creek branch that ran off from the river. Matter of fact, when we had that drought ten years back and the water level in the reservoir was down you could see the stone steps that led up to the front office of the mill. He made a good thing of it. The mill stayed in the family for a few generations, till it burned down around 1850. By that time they had another mill up in Smith's Village— cotton one. Made satinets, cotton warps, that kind of thing. Jediah's son Ezra had started a store. You know, everything from molasses to nails. Couple of Earlys by this time had served as preachers in the church.

"Now it might seem strange to you, but life doesn't change that much over the years once a family settles into a spot, a town like Enfield, a small town in a relatively isolated valley. Families tend to keep doing the same thing. As far back as I can remember there was always somebody in the cotton and wool mill business in my family, and there was always someone pastoring in the church. If it wasn't an Early it was a Hayes, if not a Hayes, a Goodspeed. Goodspeeds came in from the Rhode Island branch."

"What about the kids?" Sam was staring into the darkness, trying to picture it all.

"For a kid there was school and chores. That's not to say there wasn't any fun. There were plenty of picnics, fishing and scallywagging—you know what that is? Doing stuff you weren't supposed to be doing. But whatever it was you were doing you didn't go that far to do it. It was all right here, in the valley, in your town, whether your town was Dana, Enfield, Greenwich or Prescott. You might go to another town occasionally. Just hop on the train, the Rabbit. They called it the stoppingest train in the country. Ran from Athol to Springfield. Nineteen stops, pretty much down the center of the valley. But for most of us everything was here. Boston seemed as far away as San Francisco. Things 'happened' in other places. Cities grew. There were disasters, world's fairs, political scandals, changed skylines—but not here, not in the valley. As I said, life in the villages remained pretty much the same.

"So when those first rumors, dim little whispers, started coming through, well, everyone's first thought was 'Oh, no. Won't happen here. Nothing ever happens here, so this certainly won't.' Then bam!" Gus slammed his fist into his hand. "Next thing you know the valley's crawling with surveyors. But still nobody really believed anything would change all that much. When you have always known one thing and nothing else, only that one thing, and your parents only knew that and their parents and so on for generations, it's hard to believe there's anything else. I mean . . . " Gus stopped. "Well, here's one for you. Do you believe in Martians?"

"What?" said Sam.

"Martians . . . or life out there. You know, little critters or whatever hopping around on other planets and stars."

"Well, I don't know really."

"That's just the point. We don't know, therefore we don't believe it could be, because all we do know is life here on earth. But just because we only know that, it seems like a pretty poor reason not to believe that there could be something else out there beyond us. Anyhow, I was talking about human beings—people in this valley. There were no demonstrations, no protests when it finally happened. Certainly nothing organized. It surprises you, doesn't it?" Sam could feel Gus turn his eyes toward him in the dark and he nodded in agreement. "Yeah, I thought it would surprise you. But those were different times back then. People really hadn't heard of protests, demonstrations, or any of that. 'Eminent domain' is a big fancy term, you know. Reeked of some kind of celestial approval, if you get my drift here. Sounds like God ordered it, not the state legislature. Sort of like Manifest Destiny. Big phrases like that help small people accomplish amazing things. So we kind of became part of it. Oh, the older folks were more reluctant, harder hit, but it was the depression. Changing a valley into a reservoir meant work.

"There were dams and dikes to be built, surveys and soil analysis to be done. Not to mention the leveling of the land. The 'woodpeckers,' the workers from Boston brought in to chop and clear every living tree, swarmed through the valley. Business boomed. My dad made more money in six months than he had in two years. But it still was hardly worth it as far as he was concerned. It was difficult for someone at his age to be forced into retirement that early, give up his store and all. He would gladly have given up those six months of profits for another twenty years of working, of having his store.

"Once I knew that there was no turning back, no stopping the Water Commission . . . " Gus paused here. "Well," his voice seemed more distant as if he were reaching far back, "well, I remember clearly when I got my first glimpse beyond what it was planned to be, to what it might become. It was early fall. The town had already officially ceased to exist some months before. Twenty-six people attended the final town meeting. Of those twenty-six, not a single citizen of Enfield, which was then owned by the state, had a dollar's worth of property in the town.

"Anyhow, the town meeting was over, and I and all of my family, along with every other citizen of Enfield, would be immortalized on a war memorial in the new Quabbin Park Cemetery. One side of the war memorial had been reserved as a tribute to the townsfolk of Enfield. But still I didn't quite believe it all. I'd gone in to help my dad with the store. Like a lot of others I had taken a job with the Water Commission. I was photographing terrain. First time I ever got to ride in an airplane. Aerial photography—very exciting for a young fellow, aspiring photographer in the middle of the depression. My dad understood, and I understood my dad—forty-eight years old, forced to shut down, too old to learn a new trade, too young to retire. We had just finished opening some cartons. I had stopped and was just looking north toward Mount Ram. That's what you saw from the porch of the store. The woodpeckers had cut everything except trees on the top of the mountains and the highest elevations. The color was starting to turn. Still a lot of green mixed in with the russets and flaming reds and oranges of the sugar maples. Beautiful sight, a New England mountain in the fall. Looks like a patchwork quilt. My dad stopped to look up too.

" 'That one going to go under?' he asked.

" 'No, Pop. Mount Ram, Big Quabbin Mountain, Little Quabbin, Pomeroy, few others—they'll be left above water.'

" 'Be islands, I guess, not mountains anymore.'

" 'Guess so.'

" 'Hmmph,' he says, getting his pipe out to pack. 'Never thought I'd see such earthly transformations. Usually takes millenniums for such geological marvels to occur.' He was silent for a while, then he chuckled low. 'Instant history! Become a relic in your own time!'

"I couldn't say much to Dad on this. Didn't know what to say really. 'We're getting extinct, Gus,' he says, 'like dinosaurs and those—what do they call them—Neanderthal men they dig up. They look at their bones and make fancy assumptions about how a creature lived, what he believed, ate, thought or didn't think.'

" 'You believe that stuff,' Dad asks, 'Elihu Goodspeed's always talking about? What's he call it, Gus?' Uncle Elihu was the retired pastor of the church.

" 'Chain-of-being theory,' I answer.

" 'Yeah, another fancy word. Go to Harvard and come back with some half-baked notions like Elihu's. Thinks that everything that makes up God's world will always be replenished. "We'll find new work, Jed," he says. "God provides. We shall find new lives, new habitats"—"habitats," he says, like we're some burrowing creatures. "There's plenty of room on God's earth for everyone." Well, all that's fine for Elihu. After all, the world is his flock and he's retired anyhow.'

"My dad could be absolutely merciless about what he called the religious fanatics in our family. Although, as you know, Sam, I am not one for organized religion on any count—I must have inherited this from my dad—I would be the last ever to call a Congregationalist a fanatic. Hell, you practically have to take a pulse on them during worship. I know. My mom was the churchgoer and she dragged me and my sister every Sunday.

"My Dad was saying stuff like, 'All that chain-of-being bunk! Doesn't Elihu know that one day we're going to use up our credit?' And he picks up a broom and begins sweeping the steps of the store. 'Your Uncle Elihu thinks everything is divinely ordained, including the Water Commission, and that Mr. Xanthus Goodnough is God's representative on earth. Anyhow, you know Uncle Elihu's notion is that first there was some lowly form of life—slugs, worms or something like that—then birds, reptiles, next thing you know there's dinosaurs. They up and died off after a few million years, conveniently clearing the way for other folks—higher life forms, like us—God-fearing Congregationalists. Hence we inherit—what is it Elihu calls it—the sovereignty of the earth. But who knows?' He paused and took a pull on his pipe. I can just see him now. There was a wicked gleam in his eye. 'Maybe it was all a mistake,' he says, 'a kind of accident, that it was us instead of the dinosaurs. Maybe so-called intelligent life is an accident!' "

Gus stopped in his narrative and shifted on the pallet. "For a storekeeper, my dad could be pretty philosophical. I took the rest of the afternoon off and decided to climb up Mount Ram. When I had to get off by myself I would often go up there. Now, it wasn't just that I wanted to think, but there was a lot of tension at home because of the cemetery thing. You might not even know about that, Sam, because people tend not to talk about it, but there was plenty of talk then. My mother wanted a preacher there when they moved the old folks' bones— people's parents and grandparents; and there was a little baby that had died a few days after being born. My dad naturally did not want a preacher. 'Who you going to get,' he'd say, 'Elihu?'

" 'Not Elihu, Jed,' my mother would say. 'We can get that new young pastor from Belchertown. Just somebody to say a prayer.'

" 'The prayers been said.'

" 'But they're digging them up—for Lord's sake, Jed!' " Gus sighed. "Round and round that argument would go. Anyhow, I took myself up Mount Ram, not just to think, but be away for a while. There was of course a lot to think about—chains of being, Congregationalist slugs, Methodist worms, digging up the dead and the sovereignty of the earth. A hefty list, to say the least.

"There was a rock outcrop up there that you could sit on and look north up the valley. Course it had all been cut now. Laid to waste. Only bits of fall foliage on top of Ram and the tops of a few other hills. The land had been uniformly destroyed up to those points. All the cut trees stacked in neat little piles like matchsticks. There were several dark smudges where the woodpeckers were burning debris and brush. I sat there and looked out and for the first time tried to imagine what four hundred twelve billion gallons of water would look like filling up this valley—to imagine Greenwich as the floor of the reservoir and Prescott as a peninsula with a shoreline, Enfield as an inlet, a kind of fjord at the southern tip. I tried to imagine islands instead of mountains, waves and whitecaps instead of stone fences, banks instead of meadows. To imagine no roads and no town greens, no more creeks tumbling, no more rivers running—just this immense body of soundless still water lying over the histories of people and places and lives, drowning out a past.

"At that moment I happened to look up and nearly slipped from my perch: A red-shouldered hawk floated out of the sky. It was not that uncommon a bird, but I hadn't seen one in years. They're a bit shy, you know. Not as shy as eagles. But that started me thinking about shy things and wild creatures and how this reservoir, this man-made sea, might become an unintentional wilderness. My dad had talked about the accident of intelligent life. Well, maybe this was another kind of accident, a little loop back in the old chain-of-being theory, out of which would come an accidental wilderness.

"I got so excited I started to tremble. I looked out and I didn't see dark smoke smudging the valley floor or the stacks of splintered wood. I saw wilderness, a forest coming down to the banks, a deep forest of hardwood—ash, oak, you name it—and coniferous trees. I imagined wet meadows, swamps and bogs; and with all that would come beaver and wood duck and mergansers and foxes and gray and red squirrels and snowshoe hare and owls and bobcat and coyote and hawks—red-shouldered and red-tailed and broad-wing and rough-legged and goshawks and osprey and loon and . . . " Gus stopped. He was so still that Sam could hardly hear his breath. "And eagles!"

TWENTY-TWO

By the time they reached gate eleven the next morning
Sam was practically carrying Gus.

"You know how to drive any, Sam?"

"Sure."

"That's right, you and the New Holland stack loader.
Think you could drive a Chevy station wagon?"

"No problem."

Sam helped Gus into the car. Gus was shaking hard
now. "Gus, I better get you to the hospital."

"No!" he barked. "Just drive me home. I'll be fine."

Twenty minutes later they were at Gus's house just off
Route 202. He had let Sam call Mildred, who was on her
way. Sam had helped him into bed and gotten medicine
and a heating pad for his back. They heard Mildred's
car pull up outside.

"I'm here!" she called as she came through the front door.

"You moving in?" Gus said. She had just put her suitcase down inside the bedroom.

"Damn right!"

Sam breathed a sigh of relief. He realized that for the last few days, since he had noticed the change in Gus, he had been worried about the old man's being alone. He had actually thought of proposing to Gus that he move in with his mom and him but was pretty sure that Gus would have refused. Why he had never thought of moving in with Gus, Sam couldn't figure out. "I'll come and stay tomorrow night."

"No, no," Mildred said. "Your mom needs you. I got the time. No one at home. I'm going to call the doctor now, Gus. Don't worry, I won't let them take you to the hospital. I promise."

"No hospital, Mildred. No hospital!" he said weakly. He was almost asleep now. Mildred motioned for Sam to follow her.

"You out at the blind last night?" she whispered.

"Yes."

"Thought so. Did you see the big eagle?"

Sam hesitated. "Yeah, I've seen her a lot."

"Well, when in the name of the Lord is that thing going to make up its mind about living here?"

"I don't know. It needs a mate."

"Well, where in tarnation can we find one for it?" Mildred pulled distractedly at her hair. She grabbed Sam's shoulders. Her fingers were incredibly strong. Tears streamed down her face. "Sam, we don't have much time." Mildred's face grew wavery, and Sam realized that he was crying too. "We're not going to save him."

"We're not?" Sam said in a small bewildered voice.

"Sam! Sam! You know that. But at least he could go happy—so happy, if only he knew the eagle was here to stay."

Had his own dad gone happy, he wondered. Sam was riding in the cab of a Hostess Cupcake truck. A sixteen-wheeler. Sixteen wheels to deliver a bunch of cupcakes! The driver had offered him one, and he sat eating the chocolate cake with the white scroll across the middle.

"Where you going in Belchertown?" the driver asked.

"Oh, you can just let me off at the Sunoco station. I can walk the rest of the way."

A half hour later Sam and Lucy were on the bus heading back toward New Salem.

"My first time on a bus," Lucy said.

"How do you like it?"

"It smells funny."

"Yeah. Guess so." No matter what Lucy said it always sounded so rich to Sam. Some words, he was thinking, are naturally nice-sounding words. He loved to hear Lucy talk about wood ducks and ponds and clouds and raspberries. She talked a lot with him now, especially when they pored over the old *National Geographics*, which would fascinate her for hours. But she could say a short, stubby word like "bus" or an absolute nothing word like "smell," and still they sounded like the most beautiful notes from a woodwind instrument.

"Is Gus really sick?" Lucy asked softly.

"Yes. He's real bad." Sam sighed. "Mildred—you know Mildred? The one at the restaurant."

"Oh, the pies—the blueberry pies, the peach- and the raspberry-pie lady!" Lucy's voice was warm and liquid now, the sounds amber like honey.

"Yeah, that's Mildred. She says he hasn't much time left."

"Time left?" Lucy looked confused.

"You know." Sam swallowed. He suddenly felt he shouldn't be talking about this with Lucy.

"No, I don't know. What do you mean?" The luminous jade eyes were wide and questioning.

"I mean, you know, just that. He doesn't have much time left."

"Left for what?" she asked, still puzzled.

"For living. He's dying."

"Dying?" Lucy echoed, as if she had never heard the word. She touched the tarnished locket that lay in the hollow of her throat.

"Yeah, you know, your body stops working. Death."

Lucy didn't respond, and they both stared silently out the bus window.

They went down to the beach by the hacking tower to wait. It wasn't long. Within a quarter of an hour the big eagle came drifting out of the east.

She lit directly in front of the two young people and tilted her head at that slight angle that Sam had come to realize indicated some kind of attention focused on Lucy. Lucy and Sam had made numerous visits together to the Quabbin, and the big eagle always sought them out. Although they had become attuned to the myriad of different attitudes and postures that were signs of the eagle's behavior, Sam still felt as he had the first time the eagle had peered through the lens at Lucy. It was as if there was still a narrow channel just between the two. He remained powerless and on the outside.

Now they both sat down cross-legged as the eagle inclined her white head toward them. They were all at the same eye level. It was too simple to say that Lucy was in the eagle's power. There was something shared that existed between them. The eagle was not just staring but attending. There was a communicative quality to the way in which the eagle moved its head in very small increments, slivers, really, of motion. Each move was sharp and precise. And Lucy always seemed to respond with a series of small slivered head movements.

As Sam watched, he grew lonely, much more lonely than he had ever felt in his solitary nights in the tent as the guardian of the young eaglets. He was a guardian of nothing here—not Lucy, certainly not this immense and strange bird. He was an outsider, yet powerless to leave. He was some small particle in the light of someone else's dream. To observe the dream, even without understanding it, was fascinating. It was like standing ankle-deep in the foam of the ocean's surf, hypnotized by the rhythmic crashing of waves. But there was always the fear that a rogue wave might catch you, that the undertow might suck you down to the very bottom, scrape your face against the sea floor, turn you upside down in a crush of moving water until you felt no larger than a grain of sand in the swirl of the frothing sea.

Although the "words" between Lucy and the eagle were not individually translatable for Sam, he began to perceive the general contour and shape of the exchange. Their motions were as delicate and precise as the movements of a sculptor's tool on the smallest and most finely detailed object. And just as a figure embedded in the object would gradually emerge, as the stone released the form and the suggestion of a head or a wing or an arm became discernible, so it was with the conversation between Lucy and the eagle. Sam had found the marks. They were not entirely different from the dark marks that had so often guided him through the night woods.

But now it was not the night woods that must be traversed. Sam knew now what was ahead, though he could not name it. It was not a place that had to be reached, but a time. The place would be the same, but the travelers, like beams of light that bend as they pass from air through water, would draw another reality into focus.

The biology text read:

> The lens is a highly refractive body which brings light rays into focus. In birds' eyes and especially in an eagle's the ability for rapid accommodation, for focusing, is extraordinary in comparison to the human eye. This capacity to adjust to rapid changes in light serves a bird as it flies over water and its strong power of near and far accommodation is especially important to eagles and other raptor birds such as hawks, falcons, etc.

TWENTY-THREE

"They know nothing about the woods! Those bow hunters, they don't have any sense. You go over to Shutesbury, Petersham, you see the platforms they build in trees to hunt from. They don't know a good tree from a bad tree. They'll drive a nail into anything. They could use those portable stands they sell for bow-and-arrow hunters, but they don't." Jonathan Taylor was a forest ranger for the Quabbin area. His lean face grew taut and darkened as he spoke. "They think they're Robin Hood! Well, they know as much about the woods as the sheriff of Nottingham, and, although they're not thieving from the poor, they *are* killing trees!"

It was as passionate a speech as had been given. But it didn't work. Ten minutes later the chairman banged his gavel. He nodded toward the two front rows of the auditorium. The seats in these rows were filled by members of the boards of selectmen from the towns adjacent to the Quabbin Reservation. "Ladies and gentlemen of the boards, an oral vote shall be taken as to whether to accept the first phase of the QUORP proposal, which would open up on a trial basis for one year the northeast corner of the Quabbin for limited recreational usage as specified in article 1, subsections 2a and 2b of the master plan. You will indicate your acceptance of this proposal with a 'yea' and your rejection with a 'nay.' Shall we proceed?"

"I'm going to keep track of this, Sam," Mildred said, taking a pencil and paper from her pocketbook. She made two columns, labeling one Y and the other N. The chairman began his polling.

"Mr. Findlay of Pelham?"

"Yea."

"Mrs. Erikson also of Pelham?"

"Yea."

"Mr. Berger of Petersham?"

"Nay."

"Miss Shute, New Salem?"

"Yea."

Within a few minutes it was over.

"Fifteen yeas and five nays—not even close!" said Mildred, the corners of her mouth turned down.

"Well," Sam said, "it is the northeast corner, about as far from the eagles as you can get. So this trial year shouldn't affect them too much."

"Pollyanna!" Mildred said looking at Sam with wide eyes.

"I know! I know!" Sam said.

"It's a foot in the door, you know that."

Jonathan Taylor had come over and collapsed in a seat beside Mildred. "Well," he said, heavily. "They've got their foot in the door. We've got to get a nesting eagle if we want to push them out. There's still a chance. I've talked to Bud Wiesner and Al Findlay—all those 'yea' guys. I know those guys. They're basically bankers. Bottom-line types. The reintroduction program has cost too much by their standards. The bottom line is an eagle, and until we've got one they're ready to mortgage the property. But they're swayable . . . if we get one bird in a nest and if it's not too late."

Ed Dopplemeyer, who had led the effort against accepting the QUORP addendum as an environmental-impact statement, wove his way through the crowds toward Sam, Mildred and Taylor, who were just getting up to leave. "Let's go to Mildred's and talk appeal," he called.

"Appeal, Ed?" asked a man near him.

"Yes, Curtis, appeal," he responded coolly.

Sam did not know Curtis, but he did know from school the two boys who were with him and obviously his sons, Curt and Lance Welles. They had always seemed okay to Sam. One was into track, the other football. But Sam was completely thrown off guard when Curt, the older one, turned to Sam and, with a definite sneer in his voice, said, "Who you going to get to lead your appeal? The American Civil Liberties Union?" Sam was stunned.

Dopplemeyer turned around to the boy. "Not a bad idea."

"What about our recreational liberties?" Lance responded. The senior Curtis laughed warmly and patted Sam on the shoulder, obviously trying to make amends for his son's rudeness. Why, Sam remembered thinking, is this man patting me on the shoulder? Instead he should be telling his creepy son to shut up. This issue was really running at a deeper emotional level than he had imagined. Two minutes before, he had thought the Welleses fairly decent. Now Lance joined in. "Going to get the A.C.L.U. to take on eagles as clients?"

Creepdom, Sam thought.

"That's enough, Lance," the father said, trying to herd them out.

"But that's a point, Dad," Curt said, speaking over his shoulder to his father. "Eagles really aren't American. At least not citizens—just symbols."

The notion of living things as mere symbols sickened Sam. "Yeah, Curt!" Sam nearly spat the words out. "You're kind of just a symbol yourself—of a Neanderthal. Better start wearing that football helmet of yours off the field to protect that symbol of a brain!"

"Here! Here!" Mr. Welles said.

"Listen, punk!" Curt wheeled around, his face distorted with rage. "People don't go around insulting me!"

Mildred's hand was on Sam's elbow, to guide him firmly toward the door.

"Yeah!" said Lance.

"You two want to beat me up? Maybe between you you've got a whole brain."

At that the younger one took a swing at Sam, but Ed Dopplemeyer stepped in and caught the blow. "Okay! All you guys shut up!" The people around them were aware now of the altercation, and it had become very quiet. "Curtis," Dopplemeyer said. "Get your boys out of here. Sam, you come with me."

"I've got a ride home with Mildred."

"Fine. Go with her now."

Sam sank down in the car next to Mildred, leaned his head back against the seat and looked up.

"I'd better start lifting weights, Mildred."

"Why's that, Sam?" She turned on the ignition.

"Because picture it next year down at the Quabbin

Beach and Recreational Center with the bullies kicking sand in this ninety-pound weakling's face."

"Now Sam." Mildred reached over and patted his knee. "Those boys . . ." She paused. "Well, I always did think the father was a turkey and I guess the kids are too. But, look, Jon Taylor thinks there's hope. A lot of people do. If only that darned eagle would . . ." Her voice tapered off. Sam had not really heard her. He was thinking of next year. His imagination had taken a doomsday turn as he envisioned the golden arches of McDonald's looming up where the hacking tower had once stood, a video arcade in the blind, Curt and Lance on surfboards, kids roasting marshmallows, somebody getting to third base with a girl under an overturned canoe on the beach. Good clean fun. Our recreational liberties defended.

TWENTY-FOUR

The phone rang early the next morning. Sam, from his bedroom, could hear his mother pick it up in her room across the hall.

"Yes . . . yes . . . oh dear!"

He was out of bed immediately and across the hall into his mother's room. Lucy was still asleep in the guest room next to Philippa's.

"What is it, Mom? Is it Gus? What happened?"

Philippa raised her hand to still his questions. "Okay . . . yes . . . But he's feeling better now? . . . Yes . . . yes . . . sure. Lucy's here. She spent the night. . . . Okay, fine. I'll bring them over. . . . Right, Mildred. Bye-bye." Philippa set down the receiver. She did not look up but stared at her hand, which was still on the phone.

"What is it?" Sam said weakly. "It's Gus. He's going, isn't he."

"Well, he had a very bad night, and the doctor's been there this morning. He's feeling a little better, but they think it's going to be . . ." She paused. Her throat seemed to be wrestling with the words, the sounds she was trying to make. She swallowed two or three times. "Th-th-they . . ." she stammered. "They think it's going to be a lot sooner than expected. He'd like to see you and Lucy this morning. He gets worse in the afternoon and needs more medication and isn't really, you know, with it, so . . ." Lucy had walked into the bedroom. "So why don't we all get dressed and get right over there," Philippa said.

Sam was scared now. "Do you think . . ." He stopped. It was so hard for him to talk about anything to do with death. "Do you think he's going to die today, Mom?"

"I . . . I don't know. Death takes its own sweet time when it wants or . . ." She stopped here. Her lips clamped into a bitter little line. "Or it can grab you in a flash."

"I'm okay," Gus said weakly as Sam and Lucy and Philippa entered his room. "As okay as one can be, considering what's going on inside me." Lucy walked directly to Gus's bedside, picked up his hand and held it lightly in her own. "Lucy," he said softly, "you're going to make me cry doing things like that." Sam watched them carefully. They did not speak, but looked directly into each other's eyes.

They stayed with Gus until early afternoon, when the doctor came and gave him a large injection. Gus grew groggy and inarticulate within a matter of minutes. It was a cool, clear day, perfect for walking the four miles from Gus's house to Sam's. So Lucy and Sam set off.

"It's almost too beautiful," Sam said suddenly.

"Too beautiful for what?" Lucy asked.

"For dying," Sam said quietly. Lucy remained silent. He probably shouldn't have said anything, but he couldn't help it. Within him there was this terrible anger. If he had a choice he would die on a lousy day, he thought—rain, sleet, snow. The black, ice-glazed highway. A storm-laced Indiana night. Lucy had begun to swing her arms freely and hum. There was a gaiety in her whole being. In a light voice she began to sing.

"No daffodils,
No fleecy clouds,
No bird upon the wing.
The company for this last trip
Are not the mates of spring.
Instead there are the black whirlpools,
Flying shards of ice.
A northeast wind storms through the race,
And numbness is the single grace
To bless a soul this night.
A scream is frozen in the brain,
A void beckons—here ends all pain!"

"Lucy!" Sam stopped in his tracks. She turned toward him, her face clear and calm as the day. "What was that?"

"What was what?" she asked.

"That song. That poem you just recited."

"I didn't recite any poem."

"You did! You just did!"

"I didn't say anything!" Her dark brows knotted over her eyes.

"I heard you!"

"I was just humming," Lucy said resolutely.

"You were humming and then you added words—a poem."

"I don't know any poems. What words did I say?"

"About daffodils and storms and ice and whirlpools." He stopped. Her brow was smooth again. Did he see the veil, the translucent veil, the gaze turning inward as the veil darkened, becoming opaque and then impenetrable? "Forget it," Sam said suddenly. "Want to learn a poem since you don't know any?"

"Sure," Lucy said, her voice lively again. "You know poems?"

"Yeah, lots. My mom's an English teacher. It's part of the deal."

"Tell me a poem," Lucy said eagerly.

"Uh . . . well, darn, now that you asked me I can't think of one." At one time he had had to memorize stanzas of John Greenleaf Whittier's "Snow-Bound," but all that he could remember now was something about apples sputtering in a row. Besides, in August why recite a poem about being snowbound?

"Come on! Come on!" Lucy urged.

"Wait a minute. I can't automatically crank this stuff out. Oh, wait!" He held up his finger. "Okay. Here goes."

> "I must go down to the seas again, to the lonely sea
> and the sky,
> And all I ask is a tall ship and a star to steer her
> by,
> And the wheel's kick and the wind's song and the
> white sail's shaking,
> And a gray mist on the sea's face, and a gray dawn
> breaking."

He stopped.

"Is that all?" Lucy asked.

"No, but that's all I can remember."

"Oh, darn! It's so beautiful. Can't you remember any more?"

"No, not now," Sam said. "Gee, I never thought I'd forget it, either, after hearing my entire English class in Kokomo recite it individually from memory. We had to learn it by heart."

"Ooh, that must be hard."

"My mom never makes kids memorize poetry. She says it kills the poem and the kid in the process. But I had Dinkleberry."

"Dinkleberry?" Lucy asked.

"He was my English teacher. Dumb as his name." Lucy laughed. "And if you really wanted to hear a poem killed—drawn and quartered, guillotined and massacred—you should have heard Hogg Wilmot recite 'Sea-Fever.' "

Sam had a hard time falling asleep that night. He would be just on the brink of sleep, then a fragment of Lucy's strange poem would tear through his brain and he would be completely awake, awake and baffled. She had said those words; yet she honestly believed she had not, had only hummed. What was the meaning of all this, weird poems out of nowhere. He remembered yesterday's encounter with the eagle. The strange feelings, the sense of a journey to be made, of travelers like beams of light that bend. . . . Sam sat bolt upright.

> I must down to the seas again, for the call of the running tide
> Is a wild call and a clear call that may not be denied.

The clock said twelve-fifteen and he knew that the time

had come. He crept into the guest bedroom and woke Lucy.

The moon was just rising as the two young people threaded their way through the woods. By the time they reached the tower it was one-thirty in the morning. Stars were cast and the Archer and the Swan blazed in the summer sky. Lucy and Sam climbed high into the August night, their silhouettes limned by the moon. They stood at the very edge of the platform facing east. Over the dark cone that was Mount Pomeroy there was a darker print against the sky as the eagle soared on the mountain updrafts. The wings began to flap as the bird passed over the cooler air coming off the water and headed for the young people who waited.

TWENTY-FIVE

There was the quick flash of the nictitating membrane as if to clear the debris of flight and prepare for a new order of vision. The eagle then fixed Sam and Lucy in her gaze again and began a rapid series of head movements. Lucy responded naturally, and now Sam too was gaining a fluency. He seemed excited in this world beyond carved sounds, the ones the humans called "words."

"Where to begin my story?" The eagle nodded in question.

"Manitoba," Sam responded quickly.

"There is as good a place as any. But that is just one beginning." The nictitating membrane swept across the eye as if other beginnings, dimmer, more distant, could be perceived.

"Begin!" Lucy urged.

The eagle looked at her. "All right, a beginning in

Manitoba nearly four and one-half years ago. Three eaglets in the nest. The nest was in a tree on a narrow talon of land that hooked out into a stretch of water. Other talons hooked into the water too. From our nest I could see three. But mostly I saw the sky. That is what you scan and search all the time as an eaglet. When parents hunt you scan the sky—hungry, waiting for their return. The excitement itself when we first spotted them drifting out of the blue air was like a wind in our nest. When they were still far away we would guess what they carried in their talons. I was best at guessing. I could see the fish scales while Noss, my brother, would be saying mouse feet! He would take a guess, a blind guess at anything, just for the sake of guessing. He was that kind, you know. I doubt if he's still alive. Zelphir, my sister, she saw well but was hesitant to comment. My name, you ask? My name is Ilirah.

"We had, the young ones, lived a cycle of one moon. It was the time of the thin bright crescent when the rest of the moon is faintly lighted. It is the time when it is said that the old moon is in the new moon's wings. Earthshine, you call it? That is one of the words humans carved? I see. I see. Well, it was at this time when the new moon's wings held the old moon that the others came. Others?" Ilirah tipped her head toward Lucy. "They were not eagles or birds of any sort and they were not prey. We had never seen any other kind of living thing. So they were just others. I learned the carved sounds much later . . . human . . . man . . . woman . . . boy . . . girl.

"We heard the others from far away. They came like no animals within our eye or hidden eye. Hidden eye?" Now Ilirah tipped her head toward Sam. "Hidden eye— it is hard to explain. It does not see the way the eye sees

175

or the same thing that the eye sees—not with the light from the outside. It sees from within, with the help of an inner light. In the beginning the hidden eye does not work that well, but it grows stronger as we grow. In the beginning the hidden eye never saw our parents when they were not in the nest. We forgot them completely. But when we gained a few weeks we could see them when they were not there. We could see their wings spread in flight, the prey in their talons. That is why we could play our guessing game.

"Imagination?" The eagle crooked her head toward Sam. "That is the carved sound? No. Hidden eye I think is better. You agree? Good.

"I was telling of the others, however, and how they came in a way that even our hidden eye had never seen. There was noise. Terrible noises. First roars from the sky and then odd wind currents as the hard birds came out of the sky and landed on the water. And then the others came out on the wings and came ashore. Always with noises—empty clanking noises on the land. Our parents of course flew off, out of the nest. They were more frightened by the sounds than we were.

"We couldn't fly yet so we were helpless. We were not really that frightened, though. Angry? Angry at what? Our parents? No! If we had had our flight feathers, we would have flown too. What would be the point of having wings if one didn't use them. No, we had nothing but admiration for our parents. To see my father sheer a *djhirinjah*—that is one of the winds—was a sight for joy, not anger. So there we were, helpless but not angry, curious, really, as to all the new sounds. Noss of course was making guesses as fast as his hidden eye could work. It was the spirit of the south wind, he said, seeking vengeance on the north, just as in the tales our mother told us. It has come to take a tall straight tree of the north and change it into a poisonous vine of the south. Zelphir and I knew that was not how the story had been told at all. Noss had it all mixed up. We were so busy arguing we did not even heed the others' approach. Then Zelphir seemed to freeze. We both noticed it at once, and Noss fell silent. They were right there! At the bottom of our tree! And we heard not just the clanging scales now but our first carved sounds. We didn't know the meanings of words. They were probably talking about us, how to reach us. Their equipment—chains, spikes—that was what had been responsible for all the noise.

"We felt the tree shake. They were coming. 'Do you think we could fly?' Noss asked—weakly, I might add. 'Are you *jraha*?' Zelphir answered with more fight than I had ever seen her show. 'Well, I remember how Mirrah and Murrah did it,' Noss said. Mirrah and Murrah were our parents. 'You might remember,' Zelphir said, 'but it won't do you a bit of good. Your tail feathers haven't readied yet.' She was right, of course. Just then the other appeared—his fur first, then the odd eyes the color of the sky. He clanked, but there was another soft sound that came from his beak area. It was soft as the lightest breeze, or *haj*, as the breezes are called, over still water. And then quickly, but so firmly, his hands were on me, on my legs. I saw Zelphir and Noss, the look in their eyes. They were stunned beyond fear. And then there was nothing. Just darkness. Out of the darkness came the other sounds, carved sounds, but with rounded edges like the warm breezes. The darkness was not bad, though. It wrapped itself around me. Then of course there were the soft sounds of the other. A second other came—the old one, the one you call Gus. His voice at first seemed rougher, but he of all of the others knew us the best. There were three other eaglets. We saw each other for the first time when they transferred us to the cages for the long trip in the hard bird.

"By the time we reached Many Waters . . . Many Waters? Yes, the carved name is Quabbin, I believe. By the time we arrived here, the thin bright crescent had grown thicker. The wings of the new moon held nothing, and I and my tower mates watched its thickening each night through the cage's clangs that striped the sky and mountains and water. Those clangs!" Ilirah dipped her head toward the bars of the hacking-tower cage. "They were nearly the end of my hidden eye. It stopped seeing. Everything grew dimmer. I tried very hard to keep the hidden eye working and the visions sharp. I would ask my cage mate, a very sulky dull fellow, if he remembered this or that. Had he ever heard the wind tales? He thought he might have. Then again he wasn't sure. How could he not be sure! I was shocked. The wind tales—every eagle knows them.

"There are thousands of different winds. We would not know them without the tales. Each wind is special, at its center a *jhur* that is always there even when the wind seems gone. So each wind is named for its *jhur*. 'Spirit,' you carve it? Yes, spirit I suppose could be similar to *jhur*. The *jhur* then becomes the wind's name. To fly really well you must know the *jhurs*, for each must be flown differently."

Ilirah then ran her beak through her feathers. "But my cage mate, this dullard, had either never heard a single wind tale or had forgotten them all. Perhaps his Mirrah and Murrah were at fault. Who knows. But Zingah, that was the fellow's name, really cared only about food. And the food, as you know, arrived twice a day on time, dropped through the hole—suckers, trout, deer meat. It was plentiful, but tasteless for me at least. I would have gladly forsaken a chunk of deer meat, bristles and all, that is dropped through a hole for a tiny mouse or chipmunk still bleeding in the grip of Mirrah's talons as she banked off the rolling edge of a *djhirrahu*, which is another of the winds. Oh, how I tried for a vision of them sheering a *djhirinjah* or riding *haj*. But the visions were fading, just as the stars seemed less bright when seen through the clangs. . . ."

TWENTY-SIX

There had been a New Year's Eve, years before, when Sam had wanted so desperately to stay awake until midnight. He had made his parents promise not to let him fall asleep. "I want to see midnight," he had told them. "I want to touch midnight." After all, it wouldn't be plain twelve o'clock. It would be the last second of the old year before the first second of the new year. The year would arc over the dark zenith of the night and disappear. By staying up, Sam could watch a year turn. He could feel the world move across one of one hundred stepping stones toward a new century. This was not to be missed. This was life! One small piece of time to be held and examined and turned over like a single precious rock that was part of an immense range of mountains. And just after the clock had struck, Sam had succumbed.

His father carried him up to bed. "Did you like midnight, little fellow?"

Now, as Sam looked at the old man struggling in his drug-thickened world, he was reminded of the little boy who had wanted to touch midnight.

"Is she coming back to nest?" Gus's voice flickered like the uneven last flame of a candle.

Sam looked across at Lucy. "We . . . ," he hesitated. "We . . . ," he began again, "we think so." Lucy returned his gaze steadily across the bed.

"Think so?" The words seemed to crumble. "Don't you know so?"

"Not for sure," Sam answered, but Gus was almost asleep.

Sam sat down in a chair, leaned back and watched Gus sink into a deeper sleep. It seemed to Sam that something about the quality, the very physical properties of time had changed in the last two days since Gus's relapse and his and Lucy's meeting with Ilirah. When they were away from the Quabbin, from the tower, time became a dense and viscous thing through which one had to paddle, like heavy water.

He then remembered that in fact there was such a thing as heavy water. It was a physics phenomenon that his father had once explained to him. Maybe this was "heavy time," dense and thick, through which Gus now had to paddle between medications and through which Lucy and he had to swim between the time in and outside of the Quabbin. Inside the preserve, on the tower platform, there was a timeless quality, a feeling of expansion and infinite space and endless reaches of starlight.

There were three times during the morning when Gus swam to the surface of the thickening sleep to ask about the eagle. Then toward afternoon he simply opened his eyes. There seemed to be a new sharpness in them. Sam waited for Gus to ask about the eagle, but he never did. The afternoon went on and Gus became more and more alert. Still, he never asked.

Finally, it was dusk. Sam sensed a change in the room as the late-afternoon sun stole through the curtains.

"Come here," Gus whispered softly. Lucy rose quietly from her chair and moved as close to Gus as she could. Sam hesitated, the old dread flooding back. Then he, too, got up and went to the bed.

Gus smiled and slowly raised his hand. Sam took Gus's hand into both of his own, holding on tightly and smiling in return.

In a stronger voice, Gus said to them, "Since that day on Mount Ram I had a dream. You both know what it was. It wasn't simple to have it, to dream—but just having one, a dream, made all the difference."

Then he shut his eyes forever.

TWENTY-SEVEN

There was a soft knock on Sam's bedroom door.

"Yes?" He looked up. Lucy peered around the edge of the door. "I'm not ready to go yet," he said in a low voice. Lucy said nothing. It had been two days since Gus had died, four days since he and Lucy had last been at the Quabbin. He could not explain to Lucy why he could not go. He could not explain to her why he sat in the middle of his bed clutching a pillow, surrounded by three others, as he did now. It had something to do with feelings of loneliness and a funny hollowness. Somehow the pillows helped muffle the hollow sounds. They were like soft dikes against the flood tides of loneliness. They were his resistance, his last defense. And right now he simply could not go to the middle of a dark woods to stand at the edge of an even darker sea and feel powerless and dreamless or, worse, the outsider in another's dream.

"Why not?" pressed Lucy. She walked quickly toward him. She put her hand out and touched his lightly, looking up through the fringe of dark lashes. Sam felt something within him give way as if he was being drawn into a channel, a stream of jade light. "Please come now," Lucy asked.

At dusk they headed through gate eleven.

The moonlight fell on their faces like silent silver rain. It seemed to pour through them. Sam's own head, the cavity around his brain, seemed bright with the moonlight. The clangs were as insubstantial as tinsel. Lucy's eyes, exceptionally brilliant this night, were slants of jade illuminated, perhaps, by the light of a hidden eye.

"Zingah was disaster on our day of release." Ilirah made small hooklike motions with her head. "Not a whisper from the old wind tales whistled through for him. A true disgrace to his species! They pulled the clangs. Nurrah in the other cage was the first out. Then came Ziam. I was third, and oh it was so *shirr-ah!* Everything came back. The hidden eye, its light never more dazzling, brought back Mirrah and Murrah. The tales streamed through me like the wind, and I soared. I glided! I rode every *haj* I could catch. But Zingah landed in the water! They had to fish him out, give him another start. The second time he fetched up in a tree upside down, hanging from a branch. Eventually he learned, but I doubt if ever he had heard a single wind tale. It shows, you know. I shall be very careful with my own young, to tell the wind tales."

Her own young. Sam raised his eyes, but Ilirah continued, ignoring him. "The first day I was so *shirr-ah* with the feelings of joy and power on my flight that I did not much notice what it was I was flying over. But by the second day I began to have a strange feeling. It was as if this country was dimly remembered, familiar in some way. Was my hidden eye playing tricks on me? But those islands had a very familiar line. Could they have been something from my previous *eir-ah?*" Ilirah paused. "*Eir-ah?* You don't understand *eir-ah?*" Sam had tilted his head slightly. " 'Life?' Well, I suppose you could carve it as life. Eagles have many *eir-ahs*, not always as eagles. Although the *jhur* is always that of an eagle, it can enter other beings.

"So. There was something familiar in the shape of these islands, but certainly not in the shape of any of the winds. I flew again and again around the cone of that one island. Sooner or later I probably would have understood it, but a peregrine falcon was riding the *djhirros* too. 'If you hunt for a *djhirrang*,' he nods as he wings by me, 'you won't find it here. It is a thing of the past!' he added.

"Now," Ilirah continued, "*djhirros* are narrow plumes of warm air that stream straight off islands after the sun has baked them long enough to warm the air immediately above. *Djhirrangs* are the wider plumes that rise from mountaintops, where the contrast between the cool and warm air is not as great. The water makes the difference. I caught up with the falcon. I could not understand how once there could have been *djhirrangs* and now there were *djhirros*. Thing of *what* past, I meant to ask him. How many years was he going back? How many *eir-ahs* past was his hidden eye seeing?

"He indicated for me to follow him. We flew straight over the water. No more plumes or streams of warm air. We had to beat to remain atop the waves of wind currents—to be expected over the water, of course. No free rides, as the carving goes. 'Remember the *djhirrabas*,' the falcon nodded to me. *Djhirrabas!* I think. The fellow must be *jraha! Djhirrabas* are those lovely warm bubbles—huge, the size of eight nests—that float up from the plains and flatlands. They are *shirr-ah* to fly! How could there have been *djhirrabas* here where now there is only water? But then it began to come back to me. I remembered an *eir-ah* not long before. The falcon banked steeply and came up beside me. 'See what the others can do?' he asked, nodding down; and then I knew for certain, and my past *eir-ah* climbed in the hidden eye as high as surely the moon climbs in the black dome of the night.

"There was a sudden illumination, as if a star had exploded, and in the brightness of that light I saw my own *eir-ahs* and all those of my kind. I went back further and further until I reached the beginnings, the very beginnings of *eir*. We are among the very oldest species. We have been shaped—evolved? yes—over a much longer reach of time than most."

And Sam saw it, saw the shape, the contours of the collective *eir-ah* as it spiraled back through millennia to the most distant reaches of time. There was a dimness, the dimness that preceded first light. "Too far back for now, Sam," Ilirah said clearly. And he was pulled forward, Lucy beside him, unseen but present. Whirls of warm air curled around him. Then he felt the warm pillow of a *djhirraba* and heard Ilirah's voice saying, "Now you know what *shirr-ah* means." There was an extraordinary feeling of warm buoyancy and effortless streaming through space.

"This valley!" Sam cried. Ilirah nodded. And indeed where the waters of the Quabbin Reservoir had once cut like two long fingers there was now a broad valley, and what had been dense woods was farmland and sloping hillsides with groves of trees. A silver river branched and forked. There were a few scattered towns with outlying villages, some on plains or flatlands, some on flanks of hills, some nestled in the shadows of mountains. At the edge of the plains were the three mountains, Pomeroy, Liz and Zion.

"This is on our route to the coast of the Salt Sea," Ilirah said. "There are too many others for us to stay for long, but we can't resist the *djhirrabas* from the plains and then the *hajs* and, of course, the *djhirrangs* off these three mountains. Every time we traveled between the Salt Sea and the valley of the Great River to the south we would sheer into this valley. It was here that I . . ."

"What is that?" Sam asked suddenly. A swirl of feathers streaked with blood plummeted out of the air. In the distance Sam heard a soft explosion.

"I was about to tell you," Ilirah's voice seemed to fill Sam's head. "I was shot. It happens, you know. I did not die then, not right then. See."

"Oh!" Lucy breathed softly.

"Yes," Ilirah nodded. "The bullet had ripped into the region of what the others call the ventral tract. A farmer found me. He took me to a doctor who dug it out. There was no anesthesia, either, I might add. Raptor clinics, anesthetics for birds, were a thing of the future. But there you can see me."

They felt themselves transported. They were now standing by the fence of a sheepfold. The fold was empty of sheep. In the middle stood an elderly man in overalls. A few feet off was a younger man. He had just taken off his suit jacket and turned to hang it on the fence post by which Lucy and Sam were standing. "Don't be concerned." It was Ilirah. They could sense her small head movements, although she herself seemed to be working hard and in pain on the end of a tether which was held by the farmer. "He can't see you."

The younger man spoke now. "She can't get any lift, Alf. Maybe by next week. It's that downward stroke of the wingbeat. She can't create enough air pressure for lift. That whole ventral area must still be sore."

"Sore! Only an other would carve sore!" Ilirah shrilled. Lucy and Sam could feel her pain and, with startling clarity, grasped the nature of the struggle. The feathers, which must press tightly together on the downward stroke, could not do so, at least not sufficiently to block air. The air pressure above and below the wing was agonizingly equal. There was no clear space above the wing. The crucial partial vacuum over the top surface of the wing, necessary to generate lift, was not there. Air clamped the tender wing, locking Ilirah into gravity, onto earth. "Never, never will I fly again. Never will a soft billow form under my wings or a smooth curve of wind slide over my sky-facing feathers. Even my talons hurt when I beat. How can air be so painful, blasting at my wings, tearing at my feathers."

"Come on, girl. Come on! It'll get stronger. Come on, spread and flap them. Don't worry about the lift now."

"He knows nothing! 'Don't worry about the lift. . . !' When was the last time he left the ground! It's easy for him to say don't worry about the lift!"

"She'll get there," the young doctor said. "Takes time."

"This doctor spends most of his time worming dogs and taking care of sick cows. He'd never even seen an eagle close up. He admitted it. It took six weeks before I could fly." Ilirah scooped her head slightly toward Sam and Lucy. The sheepfold had faded. The image of Ilirah on the tether vanished. "But it would be a year before I could sheer off a breeze and truly feel *shirr-ah* again. I would be shot again, several years later, and that would finish this *eir-ah*."

"But why?" Sam scooped his head slightly, and like a thousand winds whispering in his ears the voices came, many of them garbled and unintelligible. But there were threads and snatches of thought that he could follow. *Baby stealers, eagles are. Never leave a newborn unattended outside on a warm day. Steal sheep too. Powerful magic in the feathers of an eagle.* The chants, the shrill stories, the bitter voices of farmers—they all whirled through the minds of Lucy and Sam. The sky rained eagles' feathers bloodied and twisting in the wind whorls of devils' tongues and rumor.

"The others' hidden eye can be a terrible thing! But that is enough of my story. The same year, in the same valley, more important things are happening." The slight, delicate gestures of Ilirah's head were becoming blurred and indistinct in much the same way a voice becomes muffled in the distance or a star begins to fade at dawn. There was the flash of a gold disk, a clearing of light as if the air and earth had been rinsed. Lucy and Sam stood in front of a store.

TWENTY-EIGHT

"It's the Earlys' store!" Lucy blurted, as she spotted the large sign over the porch. She slammed her hand over her mouth, but the man had not heard her. He continued sweeping the steps, looking up as a younger man came down the street, carrying a heavy leather bag over his shoulder.

There was something compelling about the features. Sam looked and looked, trying to understand the pattern. The parts were familiar, but the whole was not clear until Sam saw the intensity of the eyes.

"It's Gus!" Sam whispered. "Lucy, look. Gus!" Sam began to walk toward the store. Gus set down the bag. The older man kept sweeping as he spoke.

"Out shootin' pictures, Gus?"

"Yes, sir, over there north of Quabbin Lake in Greenwich where the tunnel's to begin and over where they're going to sink the first shafts. Mapping is still incomplete."

As Sam listened to the young Gus, he desperately wanted to reach out and touch him. But Gus and the other man continued to talk, oblivious of their presence.

"Are you doing any pictures of property?"

"I told you I won't do that, Dad," he said with more than a slight irritation in his voice. "You can't evaluate a house from a photograph. I told Hammond that and so did Bud. Those folks in Boston are going to have to get off their butts and get out here themselves to evaluate."

"Well." Jed Early stopped sweeping. "I don't know if they'll listen. See today's *Springfield Union?*"

"No," said Gus, reaching for one from the rack. He began to read it out loud in a low voice. " 'Under circumstances as dramatic as any in fiction or in a movie epic, the town of Enfield passed out of existence at the final stroke of the midnight hour.' " Gus's voice grew softer. Soon it was a mere whisper and then nothing as he continued to read in silence. Sam and Lucy walked up to read over his shoulder. The dateline of the story was—1927. The article continued: "A hush fell over the town hall. . . ."

"Huh!" Gus muttered. He folded the paper and slapped it down on the porch railing of the store. "Bad news all around."

"What else?" his father asked, looking up.

"Oh, some idiot went and shot an eagle over on the Greenwich plains by Skinner's place. Old man Skinner found it."

"Dead?"

"No. Got her in the wing. Doc Brady's there now. Operated. Says he thinks she'll be able to fly."

"Now, who'd go do a thing like that?" Jed shook his

head and picked up his broom again. "It's not like we're infested with eagles around here."

"No, matter of fact, I haven't seen any riding those thermals for a couple of years," Gus said.

"Hummph!" muttered Jed. "Well, help me in with that new delivery out back. One thing that's not going to be hurting for the next few years is business. Not with all those Water Commission people setting up camp around here. I tell you one thing. I wish I sold beer. Those woodpeckers like their beer. Must work up a powerful thirst razing buildings and chopping trees."

"Let's walk around," Lucy said, and pulled on Sam's sleeve.

"Wait a minute!" Sam sank down on the steps of the store.

"For what?"

"Lucy, do you understand anything that's happened in the last . . ." He paused. He had been going to say the last hour. But had an hour passed? Or days? Or years? Conversing with Ilirah had been one thing, exchanging thoughts and feelings, learning about her life or lives. But this was something else. Ever since Ilirah had been shot, with that one shot, it was as if the sky had split open and time had been fractured.

"Last what?" Lucy asked.

"Lucy, that paper said it was 1927. Something's happened. These people . . ."

"You mean Gus and his father?"

"Well, yes, and look next to me." A small boy in knickers had just come out of the Earlys' store with an all-day sucker, sat down beside Sam and started to lick the candy. "This kid, look, he doesn't hear us or see us. Have we become ghosts or something?"

"Never!" Lucy exploded angrily. "How could you ever

say that? I've never felt more alive in my life." It was true Lucy did seem to possess a new vibrancy. Her color had deepened. Her movements, always graceful, seemed to have a crackling energy. "If you want to sit and watch this boy lick a lollipop, you can. I'm going exploring."

Sam got up to follow her and they walked together down the road.

"Where do you suppose we are?" Lucy asked, calmly looking around her.

"Enfield, I guess," Sam replied. "That's where Gus said their store was."

There were a number of people out that morning and everyone seemed to be discussing last night's town meeting.

"I won't sell for under three thousand."

"You won't buy anything in Belchertown for under five thousand." Two men were talking in front of the Swift River Hotel.

"Don't rush to sell, anyway. There's going to be lots of money to be made from the Water Commission folks coming in here and living. I've had to put on extra help here at the hotel already."

Sam found it rather boring to listen in on conversations he could not enter.

"How far is it up to Smith's Village?" he wondered aloud.

"A mile, no more," Lucy answered quickly.

How did she know, Sam wondered, but decided not to question.

The walk was pleasant, the air dry. The smell of new-mown hay was everywhere. Along the road grew sprin-klings of field flowers that had crept in from the meadows on either side. Cowslip, devil's paintbrush, daisies and larkspur embroidered the edges where the road met the field. There was the occasional turnoff that led to a deep, shady glade near a bend of the river, but Lucy seemed to prefer staying on the road. A large building appeared ahead.

"Big factory of some kind," Sam said.

"Mill," Lucy responded dully.

"Looks boarded up, though." They were abreast of the mill now. The roar of the water from the east branch of the Swift River was deafening. "Must be incredible water power. No wonder they built it right here." He had to shout over the roar. When he turned around, however, Lucy was not there. She was walking quickly, resolutely up the road. Her chin jutted out. Her eyes fixed firmly ahead. "Don't you want to see Smith's Village?"

"Not much to see," Lucy said curtly.

Indeed most of the town seemed like the mill, closed down and boarded up. A few people could be spotted, but they were deep in the business of packing—packing and forgetting. They worked with an intense self-absorption, blindly cramming bundles into wagons and piling them atop cars. A piece of newspaper used for wrapping blew into Sam's path. *Springfield Union*, May 1928. 1928! "Lucy!" Sam said, touching her on the shoulder. She had stopped in front of a neat clapboard house and was watching the family pack up.

"What?" She turned to Sam.

"Lucy, look at this." He thrust the newspaper in front of her.

"Yes?"

"Lucy," Sam said. "The date on this paper is May 20, 1928. We've walked a mile and gone a year!"

"Sam, it doesn't matter! Time isn't time anymore." She paused. "Look at this poor woman." The woman had just come out the kitchen door of the house. She was carrying a box as one might carry a newborn child, with ineffable tenderness—as though she were holding a small and precious life in her arms. Slowly she turned and looked at the empty house, as if trying hard to believe that lives had been led there, started there, ended there. There was a loud explosion. The man turned to his wife. "Come on, Lily, let's go. They're blasting for the tunnel. Thought they weren't starting till tomorrow. Guess it's today."

"It must be the Ware River tunnel," Sam said to Lúcy.

"How do you know?"

"I read about it. They had to dynamite two hundred feet of bedrock to make an aqueduct between the Ware River and Wachusett. That was the first step in getting water—impounding it for the reservoir."

The family had pulled away in their car. Lucy walked over to a stone-ringed bed of pansies, petunias and sweet William. "Look here," she said, picking up a small wooden object. "It's a baby's rattle."

"Let's go," said Sam.

"Look at that orchard down there beyond the house." Drifts of apple blossoms swayed in the air. The fleecy white of the blossoms was so thick that it obscured the branches. "Come on!" Lucy cried gaily. "Let's run through them. It'll be like flying through clouds—sheering the *djhorrahs*!" She laughed.

He saw her run down a velvety green slope toward the orchard, the dark tumbles of hair bouncing madly. She disappeared into the clouds of apple blossoms. He could hear her voice calling, "Come on! Come on!" as he was running after, leaping a low stone wall, dodging a sudden burst of daffodils. But as he approached, the blossoms began to melt away, like snow on a warm sunny day.

Soon the orchard air was spun with gold light, the leaves of the nearby maples deeply burnished, and Lucy stood quietly eating an apple. She looked up. "Got to be quick around here." She smiled, reached up and picked another apple, then handed it to Sam.

They walked up the orchard lane eating their apples. The lane joined the main road. In the distance they saw a curl of dark smoke. "That must be the smoke from the Rabbit," Sam said.

"What rabbit?"

"The train. That's what they called it, the one that ran down through the valley. Stops at all the towns. Let's see. It's heading this way. It must be going to Greenwich. Want to ride it?" A shadow of hesitancy clouded Lucy's eyes briefly. "Come on. It'll be fun, not to mention a free ride, thanks to our invisibility."

"Okay." Lucy smiled.

"Let's run. We should be able to catch it."

They ran down the main road toward the center of Smith's Village. At the depot there was a crowd of people. "I didn't know there were this many people in the valley, let alone in Smith's Village," Sam said.

"Look." Lucy pointed to a poster that read,

LAST RUN OF THE RABBIT—SEPT 14, 1935.
JOIN US FOR A FINAL JOURNEY
THROUGH OUR BEAUTIFUL VALLEY.

Lucy and Sam got on the train. There was not an empty seat. So they stood, although it occurred to Sam that he and Lucy probably could have sat on people's laps and they would never have noticed. At first there was a great deal of noise, bantering, singing, pointing out of various landmarks. Clutches of woodpeckers could be seen working, as they cleared the land. At one point a large group of bare-chested men, their ropy muscles glistening in the autumnal light, were operating large earth-moving equipment—steam-shovels, bulldozers. Some were using shovels, but they were not doing the serious digging, as one man pointed out. "Caisson work," another said.

"Naw, naw. That's where the baffle dams are going to go. When the reservoir is filled this will connect Mount Zion to the mainland near the intake shaft. Of course Mount Zion won't be a mountain then. It'll be an island."

The voices of the passengers grew quieter. The banter subsided. A hush settled on the train, and Sam studied the passengers' faces. For the first time they were envisioning their valley flooded with water—its velvety slopes a rim of mainland, its mountains turned into islands—Greenwich itself providing the floor, the very deepest part of the reservoir. Suddenly the conflagration of autumn color that had blazed atop the mountains and hillcrests was gone. Every leaf was gone. The branches, bare and black, stuck out like the limbs of skinny, spindle-boned children. Dark puddles and ditch water reflected nothing. The sky grayed and the sun hung in it like the dim, clouded eye of an old person. "I'm cold," Lucy said, beginning to shiver.

"Look, someone left a sweater." Sam reached for it on an empty seat. "Everyone's gone! Where did they go?"

"I don't know," Lucy said, putting on the sweater. "But we're stopping."

The train had just pulled into the Greenwich station. Lucy reached for Sam's hand and grabbed it tightly. Her hand felt small and fragile in his. This was the first time that Lucy had not charged ahead, full of confidence and that robust energy that had propelled them through the valley and in and out of years and months and seasons.

Sam led Lucy gently down the stairs of the train. Just as they stepped off, it began to move away. Within seconds it had simply vanished, melting into a fog bank where the tracks dipped on the route to Dana. The roar of the east branch of the Swift River filled their ears. Three old mill buildings were clustered on the banks of the river. A weathered sign over one building read

WINSHIP AND HODGES CO.
SATINETS, COTTON WARPS, SILK & PURE WOOL.

They kept to the road, both walking silently. Something seemed to draw them along, but this time it was not any energy that emanated from Lucy. The two young people were pulled as iron filings are drawn toward a magnet. They saw no one in the town center. There was only the roar of the dark river, and more empty mills. The vertical drop of the river at this point was the steepest in the valley. The power available was immense as the water blasted down the race, a thirteen-foot drop, and was churned through the blades of the various waterwheels. Although the town was empty, it seemed from the roar that every wooden gate to every headrace that led to every waterwheel was wide open and the wheels were operating at full speed. Sam had never experienced such a crushing sound in his life. It seemed beyond hearing. It simply filled him, his body and his entire being. They continued to walk straight, looking neither left nor right. Once past the mills they could feel the grip of the roar ease. Sam felt Lucy's hand relax in his own.

The road veered from the river and led into a more expansive landscape. The Greenwich plains lay before them. The sky was heavy with low-rolling gray clouds, but just beyond a hillock to the east the clouds thinned. The sky seemed bleached, and a small canyon of clear light appeared. They cut off the road onto a smaller one that led toward the hillock. Tiny, dark, cipherlike figures stood out on the hill's crest against the sky. As they walked toward the foot of the hill they saw trucks, and then the rectangular pits open and gaping. Gravestones were loaded on truck beds, coffins were stacked. Farther up the hill a group of men stood with shovels, mostly idle. Stone markers still in place in this part of the cemetery were thin and dark with age. The men's backs were turned to Sam and Lucy, their voices a low rumble. Lucy and Sam walked by, past the pallet that held a few thinned markers, beyond the shallow pits, to the northwest corner of the graveyard. Here, under a last small grove of maples, a few stones, still upright, marked some of the older gravesites. The wind came in shivers over the hilltop and through the maples. Sam felt Lucy's hand grow cold in his. With her other hand she touched the tarnished locket around her neck. Then her hand slipped from Sam's and the other dropped the locket. The stone in front of them was worn smooth and dark, as if polished by decades of winters. The inscription, although faded, was still legible:

LUCY SWIFT

1880–1892

REST IN PEACE.

There was a sudden wingbeat and a flash of white tail feathers from the stand of trees as Ilirah lifted on the wind and soared toward the canyon of light in the winter sky.

TWENTY-NINE

"Lucy! Lucy!" The name tore from Sam's throat. He felt himself spin, the sky spin. He reached out to grab something, anything—a gravestone, a hand, a branch. His fingers clamped on the strut that ran from the edge of the hacking-tower platform to the cage door frame. Slowly Sam turned around, grabbing the iron bars with both hands, and fell on his knees. He looked through the bars at the empty cage, and within himself he felt a dark void well up and engulf him. "I am alone," he whispered, "all alone." Tears streamed down his face. Alone in this world, he thought. Alone in this pocket of time. "This cage of time!" he cried, holding the bars.

He crawled into the cage and crouched in a back corner. He buried his head on his knees and waited for nothingness. But nothingness would not come. So finally he left. He climbed down the ladder and walked numbly through the dark woods. The moon was gone. The stars had vanished. There was no light in the Quabbin.

By the time he reached home it was close to midnight. Philippa he remembered was at Aunt Nez and Uncle Albert's for a party. Sam went straight up to bed. Once out of his clothes he began trembling uncontrollably. The horrible roar of the mill coursed through him once more. "What is happening to me?" he whispered, as tears streamed down his face. Maybe he had dreamed it all. Yes, yes. A strange dream. But a sweet syrupy voice echoed in his head and mocked him with the lyrics of an old song, "A dream may come true. . . ." Cinderella. Lucy was not as lucky as Cinderella. No pumpkin coaches for her.

As he was making his way through his second turkey sandwich and third milkshake, he heard his mother coming up the walk to the kitchen door. If she says I look like a ghost, Sam thought, I might just have cardiac arrest on the spot.

"You still up?" Philippa asked as she took off her wrap.

"Ummm," Sam nodded, with a mouthful of sandwich.

"I'm exhausted," his mother said. "I'm afraid I'm going to have to go straight to bed. Lucy went back to Belchertown, right?"

"Yeah, right," Sam answered, keeping his eyes on his sandwich. "Party fun?"

"Yes. You know, Nez and Albert can really be quite charming."

Sam, who had just taken another huge bite, nodded grossly and rolled his eyes.

"Don't make fun, Sam. They like you a lot."

He swallowed. "I like Nez. It's just that Uncle Albert

and I . . . well . . ." He jerked his head. "I don't know. We don't have that much in common."

"Well, blood's thicker than water, Sam." She paused and looked at him sharply. "Sam! Do you have a nervous tick? You keep jerking your head around."

"No! No! Just a crick in my neck." He rubbed his neck convincingly.

"Well, good night." Philippa yawned. "I'm beat. Don't be long."

He would be as long as it took, and it took a long time. The bike ride over to the Quabbin Park Cemetery took over an hour. By six-thirty the next morning Sam had examined only half of the nearly sixty-five hundred gravestones, and he had not found a marker with that unbelievable configuration of letters: "LUCY SWIFT, 1880–1892, REST IN PEACE." Just as his mother came into the kitchen to fix breakfast, he rode up on his bike.

"Out for an early-morning ride," he said as he came into the kitchen.

"Beautiful day for it," Philippa said as she set her coffee down. "You look pale as a ghost! And you have circles down to your chin. Why didn't you sleep in? I hope you're not coming down with anything."

"I wasn't really sleepy." The ghost reference didn't even faze him. An hour later he was back on his bike pumping toward the cemetery. By the middle of the afternoon he had looked at every stone, and had not found one with the name Lucy Swift.

Now he really was tired. He literally had not slept one hour in the last twenty-four.

"Sam, are you all right?" his mother asked at dinner.

"Just tired."

"I do think you're coming down with something."

"Maybe."

Philippa reached over and felt his forehead. "You don't feel warm, but why don't you go to bed. You really don't look so great."

"Yeah, I think I will."

As Sam walked upstairs he thought of everything he was coming down with—a ghost for a friend, another friend who had died an old man and returned to him young, an eagle who . . . Sam paused in his thoughts. An eagle who did what? Peeled away time as if it were the layers of an onion. Transported them back through time by a strange conjoining of mind and consciousness. But it was not a consciousness, he thought as he pulled off his socks. Was it a super or cosmic awareness that took them beyond physical borders into infinite space? What did it all mean?

Life had been considerably simpler when he was driving a New Holland stack loader picking up bales of hay. One, two, three, four and you were a third of the way down the row, eight more to go. Then you were at the south fence, your hand riding easy on the pickup stick. You swung round to the next line of bales. There was soft rock in your ear, and at noon you'd quit. Go down to Gram's kitchen. There would be a plateful of sandwiches. Grandpa would be there drinking hot coffee no matter how hot the day was and dipping his sandwich into the coffee. "Mutilating it," as his gram would say. As soon as Sam would sit down his gram would uncap the orange soda, fill his glass halfway up and plop in a big scoop of vanilla ice cream. She'd set it down in front of him and say, "Here you go, Sam." Four of the most ordinary words in the English language, short, flat, unmusical words, and they sounded so darn good, so positive. People like Gram never had to say the other words, like "I love you," "I believe in you" or "You're wonderful." The way she said "Here you go, Sam" was enough to launch a person for life.

He woke up suddenly, not sure how long he had been asleep. He groped for his watch. It was two A.M. He felt rested and calm. He sensed that his mother was not asleep and got up and walked to the window. There she was in the garden, kneeling on the moss. She was between the mound that Lucy had made, the small replica of Mount Pomeroy, and that boulder next to the long flat rock which by day looked like another mountain and by night, sculpted by shadow and moonlight, became the figure of a girl kneeling beside a stream. Two kneeling figures— one of flesh and one of stone, one absorbed in the gentle work of easing growth, her body curved toward the earth as she worked; the other figure bent toward the stream of the flat rock, kneeling in question, as if to seek a lost reflection within the water.

I have lost Gus, Sam thought quietly as he looked down on the garden. I have lost Lucy. I am bound to this life, this time; but maybe Lucy's life or death was an error. Gus had lived a whole life within his time. But Lucy had known only a fraction of hers, moments spent in twilight, he sensed, in a dimness of human affection. "I am going back," he whispered. This time he would be alone.

THIRTY

The sun was just setting as he and Ilirah completed their greeting. Low-angle golden light scattered across the water. As the sun sank closer to the horizon, the odd refraction of its slanting light made it seem to flatten and elongate until it was an oval, streaked with blue-gray clouds. As Sam looked toward the setting sun two bright spots, like small mock suns, appeared on either side. Sundogs, he thought. But that would be impossible. Sundogs were due to refractions of sunlight by ice particles high in the atmosphere. The sunlight was not high; the sun was sinking in the west. It was September.

"Time, Sam!" Ilirah nodded. "You are a keeper, a sentry of minutes and days and months." She dipped her head slightly toward the sun. "There was a time before time, before seconds, before minutes, before days."

The sundogs had vanished, and where the sun had just set, three bands of what appeared to be fog rose steadily. They began to glow brighter until they streamed like wind ribbons above the water. The sky was still light, but Sam was witnessing an unimaginable event—an auroralike seizure of the heavens at twilight. The windblown ribbons of light and color sprayed and coiled into ghostly configurations—rayed arcs, curtains, flames. Once again Sam's head seemed translucent and bright, this time with the extraordinary auroral light of the sky.

The world suddenly looked very odd. It was as if Earth and the entire galaxy had been compressed into a tiny circular window. Sam felt as if he could see around the curves and bends and corners of things. He felt no apparent motion, but guessed that he must be traveling close to the speed of light. Absolute time, absolute space crumbled.

They were now over the sphere of Earth. It appeared to be entirely covered with water. Sam's focus became clearer and he scoured the turbulent sea for land—any mass or configuration. He noticed an irregular shape that bore a vague resemblance to the head of a bull with its two horns. The waters seemed to be receding. Land masses broke from the sea. Two large masses seemed to drift toward each other, their shapes familiar. A crucial geological event was taking place, and Sam felt as though he were peeking over the rim of the universe and watching the Earth caught within a most ancient era, the fold between two periods. The two land masses continued toward one another on a collision course. Sam recognized them as Africa and North America. He watched them collide as if in slow motion. Land crushed and buckled on impact. Crusts of earth folded upon themselves, rocks were compacted into massive mountain ranges. An ocean retreated. This folding and faulting of the earth's crust—was this, Sam wondered, what geologists had called the Acadian orogeny?

"Words carved by others." Ilirah dipped her beak slightly. "This was before there were eagles, and there were no names for things. Watch now."

On the eastern side of the North American continent there were many valleys. The mountains around one valley were exceptionally high and began to wear away. Sporadic volcanic eruptions spewed rocks. Sam caught sight of a new mass, its blue edge moving slowly toward the valley. The glacier, its course deliberate, scooped out the valley floor as it moved through the remaining hills. The shape of the valley was recognizable. The river! He saw it now for the first time. Its east, west and middle branches spread like silver ribbons through the lush terrain.

There began to be movement other than the buckling of land and the crushing of rocks. Life was flourishing, but it was miniscule compared to the geologic upheaval he had witnessed. Unaccustomed to the smallness of scale, he missed evolutions of entire species. From trilobite to dinosaur to Ramapithecus and Homo sapiens was one regrettable blur fogging imagination, eclipsing the hidden eye.

"Concentrate!" Ilirah nodded deeply. The disk flashed in her eye as the membrane made its diagonal traverse. Sam himself blinked. The light was clearer. Details stood out. Human figures, the color of dark clay, moved through the valley.

He could feel speed now, not that of light, but a slow, steady, drifting speed, as if they were moving through water or air. Then, he was standing in a grove of birches at the edge of an Indian encampment. The Indians moved quietly as they worked, smoking meat, scraping hides and making or mending tools. Nearby, a mother crooned to her baby. Sam did not understand the words, but the shape of the song, the meaning, he somehow comprehended. The mother set her baby down on a woven mat and walked away to stir something in a pot hanging over the fire. Sam moved closer to the sleeping infant and, leaning down, he gently stroked the golden chubby curve of its cheek. The baby didn't cry, but Sam felt an inexpressible grief well up within him. His last thought was that he, like this baby, had known the shape, the warmth, the very texture of human love. That was all one ever needed. He touched the golden cheek again.

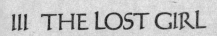

III THE LOST GIRL

THIRTY-ONE

Sam was no longer standing in the grove of birches, but beside a clapboard farmhouse. It was dark. The few trees near the house were bare.

A soft yellow light poured out the window of the house. Sam was drawn toward it. The glass of the window was thicker than any glass that Sam had ever seen, but through its whorls and imperfections he could see a group of people gathered in a tight circle. Their heads were bowed as if they were focusing intensely on something. Most of their backs were turned, but the people all appeared old. There was not a single head that was not gray, a single back not curved and bent from the weight of years. Sam moved closer until he was right up against the window. One pane of glass was missing, the space patched with paper that had been saturated with some kind of grease or oil. Through it, fragments of conversation could be heard. At first the voices were an inarticulate mumble, but he listened hard and words began to emerge.

"Collicky . . . Cries quite a bit . . . Happy too . . . Trudy? . . . No . . . No. . . ."

"Poor baby girl. . . ." Those words came from a small, round woman with barely enough hair to cover her head. "Mama gone and now this!"

"How come Trudy's kin don't come for her?" asked a bent man resting on a cane.

"Too far. Never forgave her for marrying Jess. Had someone all picked out for her in Manchester."

"Well, what in the world do we do now?" said another woman.

"We're all too old to take this on." A thin-lipped woman with pewter gray hair spoke emphatically. Sam guessed she was the youngest at fifty or fifty-five.

The small woman looked up, her faded eyes sparkling with anger. "Emmawilla, you have always been too old for anything—skipping rope, having fun or loving. It doesn't surprise me a bit."

"Now, Eliza!" A man patted the old woman gently on the shoulder. Turning abruptly, Emmawilla had walked toward the window and looked directly out. Had Sam been visible to her she would have been staring directly into his eyes. But he was not, and he used his advantage to scrutinize the face in front of him. Pinched, bloodless and grim it was. The lips were pressed into a rigid gray line, the cheeks sunken, the blue-gray eyes cold as glaciers.

"Never could believe that you and Jess shared a drop of blood," Eliza continued. While the others were hushing her and trying to mollify Emmawilla, Sam saw Eliza bend over into the middle of the circle. She straightened up slowly, and when she was as erect as her worn back would allow, two liquid jade eyes peeped over her shoulder and looked straight through Emmawilla to Sam.

Outside the old woman's bedroom window the buds ripened in the early April sun. She watched this slow swelling promise of spring and felt her own life ebbing from her. A budding branch in April is a precious thing, she thought. The small child, no more than two, stood solemnly by her bed. Eliza Swift Reid ran her fingers lightly through the thick, dark ringlets. Tears coursed down her face, following the wrinkles and creases that scored her cheeks like old riverbeds run dry. She shouldn't let the dear child see her crying. Since birth she had been cared for by a dying old lady. She never seemed to have minded or noticed the sour smells of oldness, the crooked body, the bleached eyes.

Eliza's tears were not for herself, but for the child, born into a family that was dying. The few members of the younger generation, the ones that should have been rising into their majority, had been cut down through illness or accident or the Civil War years before. And this child, orphaned at six weeks, was now to be orphaned once more. All that was left for her were the bitter ragtag ends of the Swift family, which shared a silver river's name. The irony! Never should one cry for the January tree, she thought, the ancient maple destined for an eternal winter, its sap frozen, its buds hard as pits. Cry instead for the bare branch in April, with swelling buds caught in the freak blizzard of spring.

Lucy followed the coffin through the door of the house.

She tried to climb into the wagon after it but was yanked down by Emmawilla. With her small hand clamped in Emmawilla's she was led to another wagon.

She stayed with Emmawilla until she was five. She was not beaten. She was not asked to do any more than her share. But she was neither talked to nor attended to in any way. Lucy was envied, intensely at first and then obsessively, by Emmawilla. She was envied for her innocence, her lack of bitterness, her vulnerability and what Emmawilla suspected to be her capacity for love. Finally, Emmawilla had to send Lucy away. For sixty years she had compressed her anger. Like the minerals in a sedimentary rock, her anger lay in thin bands; but now she felt that she actually might crack. She had begun having terrible nightmares, dreams of violence.

She sent the child to live with her elderly cousin Llewellyn, pleading that the severe headaches which she had always suffered had grown worse and the child's noise bothered her. It would not bother Llewellyn. He was deaf. Llewellyn died within a year. For four months Lucy stayed with his sister Priscilla. But Priscilla always spent winters in Boston with relatives of her deceased husband, and she certainly could not impose on them by asking them if a small child could come too. So finally it was arranged that Lucy should be rotated throughout the year among various people in the valley: Priscilla in the fall; Madge, Llewellyn's housekeeper, who was approaching eighty herself but needed a boarder to help pay for firewood, in the winter; Vena, a cousin of Priscilla's, in the spring; and Charles, Llewellyn's older, richer and slightly addlebrained brother, in the summer.

Lucy liked Charles the best. He was not deaf and he did talk, although sometimes he spoke gibberish. But he loved to fly kites, which she adored. Sometimes, however,

Charles looked at her in funny ways which made her feel uncomfortable. This usually happened if he had more than his customary single glass of brandy in the evening. If she would say something quick or silly, just anything really, it would break the mood and he would seem normal again. Well, not normal really, rather apologetic, slightly hangdog like an animal that had misbehaved in some way.

When Lucy was staying with Charles she would help with his medicines, which were complicated. Otherwise, Emmawilla had to come three times a week to measure out precisely the various liquids. Particularly, if Charles took too much of the green fluid it could cause heart fibrillations. Dr. Crown said he must never drink brandy on those nights. That would cause certain death. So Lucy managed the medicines during the summer and hid the brandy on Tuesdays, Thursdays and Sundays.

The best days of all were those summer ones when the wind was nice and steady out of the northwest and the sky a very deep blue. She and Charles would pack the kites and a picnic lunch and head out of Greenwich toward Mount Pomeroy. The green flanks of Pom would be stippled with daisies and wild strawberries. They had fashioned the loveliest kites, gay with colored streamers. Charles thought nothing of sacrificing an occasional curtain of a room long closed, a coverlet of a bed never slept in or even an old gown of his dead mama for the purpose of touching the sky. "Dear Mama will be so pleased to see this again!" he would shout as he threw the kite on a draft of wind and Lucy ran with the spindle of string. Lucy was not sure that dear Mama would be all that pleased to see her maroon grenadine skirt and the ruching from an old gown cut in strips and flying in the wind. But it was so much fun, and all the other children on the mountain were drawn to the beautiful kites like bees to honey.

Her very happiest memories would always be those of running barefoot down the west slope of Pom with a kite string in her hand, her palm-leaf bonnet flying out behind her. She knew the instant the wind claimed the kite. There would be the slight tug on the line, the wonderful reassurance that the kite was now floating merrily on an updraft. Slowly she would walk up the slope again, reeling in the string or letting it all out, and the kite would catch every billow and draft as it climbed high in the sky—high as Auntie Eliza or her own mama and papa whom she had never known. Oh, she was sure they were up there. And they didn't wear crowns or halos or angel wings like Aunt Priscilla always said. No, no. They were very young. At least Mama and Papa were, and she was fairly sure that Auntie Eliza was probably young by now too and had lots of hair and teeth. They all sat on clouds and hiked up their skirts and trousers and dangled their bare legs and bare feet over the edge and fished for whatever it was people fished for when they were dead and sat on clouds and looked down and probably made a lot of funny jokes about Earth. When Lucy sent up her kite and she saw it sail off into that impenetrable blue, it was just like sending a letter to the very best people in the whole world.

But then suddenly there were no more picnics on Mount Pom, no more beautiful kites sailing on breezes. Cousin Emmawilla stood before her.

"Priscilla has decided to stay in Boston year-round." Her mouth was a firm line. She might have been reciting a list of errands to be accomplished in the village. Lucy's heart thundered in her chest. "Vena feels that the five or six weeks you spend with her in the spring hardly make it worthwhile your staying on here."

Lucy's brain seemed awash with confusion. "What do you mean staying on"—she swallowed—"here?" She whispered the word. She knew they were not talking about anyone's house now. Could Emmawilla mean the valley? But the valley was all that she had ever known.

"We think you should go to work in the mills—Lowell, perhaps, or Amoskeag. We could provide you with a letter to Smythe's Mill in Lowell."

"But . . ." Lucy was stunned.

"But you are twelve, almost thirteen now." Emmawilla could still have been talking about the weight of a bag of flour, a measure of sugar. "It is time you earned your way."

"But . . ." The words came to her in a rush now. "Why Lowell? Why not Enfield, or here or Dana? There are mills in this valley. And what do you mean, five or six weeks with Vena? I spend the winter with Madge and the summer with Charles."

"Oh, didn't I mention it? Madge's niece from Springfield is moving in with her and she no longer needs a boarder."

"Well, what about Charles?"

"Oh, no, out of the question. He is becoming much more vacant and absentminded than ever. Dr. Crown thinks it not a good idea at all your staying on with Charles."

"Who will manage his medicines?"

"I can, naturally, and Madge. We do it when you're not there."

"But why Lowell? Why not here?"

"Oh, the wages are much better in Lowell, Lucy, and

you'll have much more of a chance to start a life of your own."

I don't want to start a life of my own, Lucy nearly shouted, but instead she cast her eyes down and spoke in a whisper. "I just don't understand. . . . I just don't understand."

Finally Emmawilla, patience in shreds, lashed out. "Stop sniveling! You're twelve years old. The next youngest member of this family is sixty-five. We have lived too long. We've had to sell off bits and pieces of property until there is hardly anything left. It isn't my fault that your father ran off with your mother, got a child on her. She died birthing you. Then he died in that fool accident. None of that's my fault, but here I am left holding the bundle. Well, dearie, there's nothing in the bag to hold anymore. We have barely enough for ourselves." She paused, looked hard at Lucy and took a deep breath. "You have your wits, your health and beauty . . ."— the corners of Emmawilla's mouth curled into tiny serpents—"which is more than any of us have."

Lucy didn't hear the rest of the tirade. She turned and left. That evening Emmawilla gave her travel money. Lucy packed her few belongings in an old hair trunk.

Three days later she stood on a bridge. The boards trembled from the surge of water below. Spray from the falls swirled about her. On the other side of the bridge was Lowell. From a distance it had looked like a papercutout toy town, flat against the sky. But now it rose dark and red with a crushing dimensionality. She had never seen so much brick, so many buildings climbing into the sky, spiking it with spires and chimneys and smokestacks. She had spent a lifetime in a cozy green valley where houses, fences and barns were constructed close to the earth for warmth and shelter from the wind. Fences curved naturally over the contours of the land. Sugarhouses were built against hillsides to let the gravity that nature provides carry sap from the gathering tank to the boiling cauldron. These were the harmonic rules of building with nature. But Lucy now stood before a city that seemed to rise like a clenched fist, shaking and challenging the sky, the heavens, even God.

"How old are you?" asked the girl who stood next to Lucy in the mill yard.

"Twelve."

"Don't tell them that. Say you're fourteen. You're tall. They'll believe you. If they think you're younger they'll just make you a doffer in the spinning room."

"A doffer?"

"A bobbin doffer. They're all children. They take off the full bobbins and replace them with empties. It's not hard work, but the lowest pay. Three dollars a week, maybe."

Were there one hundred spindles, one thousand, ten thousand in Smythe's Mill? It was as if she had stepped directly into the body of some enormous beast and could hear the workings of its organs. The din was overwhelming as row upon row of spinning frames sucked in miles of thick cotton rope, called roving, from the scores of bobbins. The room throbbed with the noise, and Lucy wondered if she would ever hear herself breathe again.

On the floor below the cotton had been carded and drawn into roving. On the floor where Lucy was to work it would be spun. One floor up in the weaving room it would be put on looms and woven into cloth. Lucy's friend Kezia, the girl she had met in the yard, was upstairs working as a drawing-in girl. There were no more than a dozen such girls, and because of her experience, three years in Chicopee, she got the job. How had she ever stood it? Lucy wondered. How would she, Lucy, stand it? Her term was to be one year. If she left sooner she would be blacklisted, given a dishonorable discharge.

The overseer led her to a pretty, foreign-looking woman who was watching three frames. "Stand here," he shouted. Lucy could feel his saliva spraying her ear. "Watch her. See what she does—and tie those curls back or you'll get scalped!" The woman turned and handed Lucy a string of cotton, motioning with her hands for her to tie back her hair. She turned a handle on the row of frames next to hers. The machine started. "Watch that the roving doesn't tangle," she shouted.

Like an insatiable iron monster, the machine began swallowing the endless ropes of roving, twisting them with a violent spinning action, and then, within seconds, spewing them out as finished yarn to be wound around huge bobbins. Clutching tin boxes, the doffers scampered barefoot up and down the rows. They were pale, thin creatures with smudged eyes. Lucy watched as one clambered up on her frame to collect the empty bobbin. She looked at the small bare feet and remembered the velvety grass on Mount Pom tickling her toes as she raced to set her kite on the breast of the wind and send it sailing into the blue sky.

The "operatives," as the girls were called who worked in the mills, were considered mere extensions of the machines they operated. Certainly, they were less vulnerable to variations in temperature than cotton, which might break in cool, dry air. To protect the cotton, the rooms in which the operatives worked were kept stifling and heavy with moisture. Winter or summer, windows were never opened. When the operatives broke for lunch they gulped their food, in much the same way the frames swallowed roving. It was as if the throbbing cadences had been forever drummed into them. They would never possess a pulse of their own, hear a natural sound again, but were caught within the screeching, whirring frictions of the iron beast.

That night in the boardinghouse bedroom that she shared with four other girls, Lucy concentrated on the noises of their sleep. These sounds were like some strange and beautiful music after the cacophony of the machines. She then tried to listen to the sounds of her own heart and blood, and they too were like a kind of rare music. She fell asleep thinking if only, if only I can keep listening to this music within . . . maybe, maybe . . .

Lucy worked through the fall and the winter, but just as winter was ending she fell ill. Her lungs filled with fluid. A racking cough shook her whole body. She willed herself to work every morning and finally one day collapsed at her frame. For six days she lay sick in the boardinghouse, feverish and delirious. On the seventh the fever broke and she felt better. The next day she went to work. By afternoon her chills had started again. Once more she fainted. Kezia helped her back to the boardinghouse. Another week she lay ill. This time when she returned to the mill there was no work for her. Her place in spinning room number three had been taken. There might be work, she was told, in the picking room downstairs in a couple of weeks, but then again one never knew for sure. There might be a shutdown if the flow of water slowed, stopping the wheel. Smythe, being an old-style mill, was totally reliant on its waterwheel powered by the river. Lucy was shocked. She thought nothing could stop the machines, nothing could unclench the hand that shook its fist at the sky. "You can try and wait it out," the overseer said. "Be cheaper for you I'd imagine to go home. Come back late spring."

"Yes, yes," murmured Lucy. And what did he imagine was waiting for her at home, she wondered. A farm with a mother, father, brothers and sisters? She walked in a trance across the mill yard and out the gate. She walked down Merrimack Street to Shattuck and between Shattuck and Market she turned off onto a smaller street that led to the boardinghouse. As she came up the steps, before she reached the door, it swung open.

"Thought so." It was Mrs. Ewing, the owner of the house, her face sour, mouth set in a grim line. Of course she would know what had happened, Lucy thought. There would be no other reason for a girl to return at this hour of the day, unless of course she had collapsed from illness. But in that case, someone would bring her. "What do you propose to do about your rent for the last two weeks?"

"Pay it, ma'am," Lucy replied, her eyes steady. "I have it in the bank. I just came back to get my account book. I'll go immediately."

"All right," Mrs. Ewing said coldly. "I'm going down to the cellar now to sort out some things. I'll be here when you get back."

Lucy went directly upstairs and packed her small trunk. Both she and Mrs. Ewing knew she would not be back. The excuse of the cellar merely provided a less awkward way for Lucy to steal out with her belongings. Mrs. Ewing watched from behind a curtain in her parlor window as Lucy turned down the short street that led to Shattuck. Lucy could feel the landlady's eyes boring into her back.

She would go back to the valley. She was, after all, an experienced operative with six months' work at

Smythe's Mill. She could work the spinning frames and could easily learn loom work to be an operative in the weaving room. Certainly the Whipple Company or the Minot Mill in Enfield would have openings. The salary would not be as much as in Lowell, but she could live with Uncle Charles (she didn't care what Dr. Crown said) and contribute more than her share by cooking and cleaning and making sure he took his medicines properly. Yes, this was best. She would go home. She was changed now, they would see it. She was an experienced operative, a wage earner. She would help them, ensure them a comfortable old age. She would be loved. She knew she would be loved and welcomed, welcomed as their helpmate now.

From Lowell to Athol she took a stage. She had just enough money left for a one-way ticket to Greenwich on the Rabbit. It was late afternoon when she climbed aboard. It had started to snow. There had hardly been any snow at all on the ground in Lowell, but as the train made its way down the valley Lucy saw that every slope and hillside was thickly blanketed. By the time she stepped off the train in Greenwich there was a blinding blizzard.

"Probably need a compass to find the folks who come to meet you," the conductor joked.

"Yes," Lucy laughed lightly.

"Take care now," he called.

It was just under a mile to Charles's house. If she followed the river she would have no trouble finding her way. Her feet were cold. Her boots were not really suitable for the depth of snow, but she would walk quickly and be there within the hour. It was Thursday, a medicine day. Perhaps Emmawilla or Madge would be there.

Walking was more difficult than she had imagined.

Once or twice she slipped but caught herself. She decided to walk closer to the river, as the accumulations of snow on its banks were not as deep, and she could move faster. The rock ledges were slippery, however, and she had to be mindful. She scanned the opposite bank of the river for an enormous maple tree. It would be about one-quarter mile upstream from the gristmill she had just passed. Then, fifty paces after that tree, more or less, would be Charles's house on the left.

The snow blew more thickly. The flakes moved wildly now in their mad dance. She scoured the opposite bank for the maple but could discern nothing. It should be here, at any step, any second. Her boots skidded suddenly on the wet snow, and she grabbed a root to break her fall. Her trunk careened down the embankment into the black water that rushed darkly on its own course through the white swirling madness. "Oh, no!" Lucy moaned. She made her way down to see if the trunk had perhaps landed in shallow water. Just as she came to the water's edge she spotted the immense shape of the tree. It arched over the river like a prehistoric beast regarding an intruder. "What happened?" Lucy said aloud as she stood staring at the massive maple, now uprooted. She had a glimmering prescience that everything for her was soon to change in an unimaginable way. She forgot her trunk and scrambled up the bank with one thought—to get to Uncle Charles.

She could see that there was a light on in the back of the house. It appeared to come from Charles's study behind the front parlor. His kite factory, he used to call it, for this was the room where he created the lovely constructions out of paper and cloth and strips of wood. "Another little fantasy for the wind," he would say upon completing one. Away from the river the footing was surer, but the snow was deep as she came through the orchard to the backyard. She slowed down, but not because she was tired. Her confidence in herself, in the welcome she had anticipated, was shaken. Without knowing why, she decided to step first to that lit window rather than go around to the kitchen door. As she peered in through the frosted pane, her breath locked.

The light within was diffuse. Figures and objects were blurred, and yet one presence melted through that pane of frosted glass: death. Charles was slumped in his rocker, his mouth hanging open, his eyes rolled white. On a table beside him was the open brandy bottle, the large goblet overturned. Standing beside the table was Emmawilla, her face oddly young. The bitterness was gone, and a slightly bemused expression played in her eyes as she looked down on Charles and the blackish slime on his cravat where he had vomited in the last paroxysms of death. Lucy reached up to steady herself. Her hand clasped an icicle that hung like a dagger overhead. It broke off. Emmawilla heard the noise and her head snapped up.

She'll kill me! Lucy thought. She'll kill me too! There was a bush just next to her. She scrambled under its snow-laden boughs. Emmawilla had come to the window. She looked up briefly at the fringe of icicles and seemed assured that the noise was just the sound of one falling. She turned her back. Lucy could see her retrace her steps toward Charles. Then the room was black. She had blown out the lamp. She will wait until morning to seek Dr. Crown, Lucy thought. It will all make perfect sense. Charles got into the brandy. What with the blizzard and all there was no way she could get help. Everyone would believe her.

Numb with fear and cold, Lucy could not think. She

could feel nothing now except terror. She could not stay. Emmawilla would kill her too. She must flee. She lurched out of the bush and headed back through the yard toward the orchard. She ran down the steep embankment and followed the river downstream. In a minute she would see the fallen maple. There was a brief letup in the blizzard. For a few seconds the antic flakes suspended their dance. The night appeared to be black satin; the snow-laden branches, lace against it. Lucy saw the maple, then felt both her feet slip.

The water gathered around her like endless yards of soft fabric, curling up around her neck and chin. White bubbles frothed around her throat like ruffles on a fine lady's blouse. She thought that it did not feel so cold, not nearly so cold as one would have expected. At first it felt as if she were skimming, flying down the black silk ribbon of the river; but as her clothes became sodden, their weight and the swirl of water began to pull her down.

She did not panic the first time she went under. The tiny white bubbles appeared like stars in the night. When she came up the air was bitter on her face. But still only her face was cold, a terrible cold that bit into her cheeks. The rest of her body was numb, pleasantly numb. Was this what it was like to die? Why not then bury her head in the black liquid billows? Was it really a sin? She had not caused the accident. To let it continue to happen, was that so bad?

She was being carried on her back now. Her face too had become numb. She could see the sky, and the stars embroidered the blackness. The snow had stopped falling. Oh, it is a lovely night, she thought. A lovely sky. The branches of the old maple sailed overhead. She could reach out for one and stop all this, but then her arms were so heavy and she was so tired. She would just dream a little, just a bit, of the kites, those kites blooming like gay flowers in the summer sky. How lovely they would look in the night sky. Pink and blue blossoms appliquéd against the black satin of the winter night. There was a sudden draft of air close to her face. She heard a stirring just above her. There was flash of white in the darkness, a jagged wing printed against the night. And then the water began to lap over her face like the gentle tongues of small animals.

THIRTY-TWO

The short life had unfolded for Sam with a clarity of detail and an intensity of feeling unlike any movie he had ever seen or book he had ever read. Yet it was not a movie or a book. And although he had witnessed this life and experienced it as a reader or viewer would, separated in consciousness from Lucy, Sam knew incontrovertibly the reality of the experience. It was not a dream. It was not a hallucination.

"Well," said the minister, looking up, "I suppose we should begin." He cast his eyes briefly toward the door in a token gesture of expectation. But no more people would be coming to mourn. No more except one. Sam strode up the center aisle.

Lucy in her homespun dress, the same one she had worn every day as an operative in the mill, lay in the pine coffin, her head resting on a small pillow. Above her left brow was a pale bruise which had been unsuccessfully powdered. Whoever had prepared the body had also combed her hair back tightly when it was still wet, but now the shorter hairs around her temples and forehead had escaped in curls and soft ringlets framed her tranquil face. The collar of her dress was slightly torn, and Sam could see the locket lying in the hollow at the base of her throat.

The minister began to speak the scripture. "We brought nothing into this world and it is certain that we can carry nothing out." This could only be understatement in Lucy's case, Sam thought, as he took a place beside Emmawilla. "The Lord gave and the Lord hath taken away."

"Except," whispered Sam into Emmawilla's ear, "when dried-up old witches like you interfere!" Emmawilla blanched visibly and swayed a bit on her feet. Sam was amazed. Had she really heard him? He knew he was still invisible. Perhaps his whisper was like some sort of subconscious or cosmic conscience echoing within her. God and Sam knew that Emmawilla certainly did not have a conscience herself.

"Blessed be the name of the Lord," the minister intoned. "Dear Lord, today thy servant Lucy . . ." The minister looked up. "Emmawilla, did Lucy have a middle name?"

"Not that I know of," she replied flatly.

"You must be getting good at this," Sam whispered to Emmawilla. "First Charles and now Lucy." She flinched again. Her granitelike composure was vulnerable, Sam knew, and he intended to chip away at it. He was motivated by a powerful blend of emotions—outrage and profound despair, the deepest sorrow he had ever known. It was deeper, more desperate than anything he had experienced when his own father had died.

If this strange time warp within which Sam was suspended, this peculiar capacity he had now for conjoining his consciousness with others, served nothing more than to provide a medium for the expression of some of his most powerful feelings, it was certainly worth it. For Sam now knew that until these feelings of his were spent, he himself would remain a cripple of sorts. That a human being should have endured the isolation that Lucy had from birth to death was incomprehensible. That her life in its brevity had become such a distillation of loneliness was profoundly shocking, an outrage that no God in heaven could explain, no religion should tolerate, no species endure. The prayers and words of the minister were meaningless—wooden sounds that knocked and banged like an unlatched gate in the wind. A vessel had been emptied of life, and now this rasping wind blew around it, mocking what had once been there.

Sam began to sing to drown out the minister's words, softly at first; but as the gentle melody of the old hymn, a favorite of his Gram's, caught him and rocked him, he began to sing it louder—for Lucy.

> "There's a land that is fairer than day,
> And by faith we can see it afar,
> For the Father waits over the way,
> To prepare us a dwelling place there.
>
> In the sweet by and by
> We shall meet on that beautiful shore;
> In the sweet by and by
> We shall meet on that beautiful shore."

His voice grew stronger.

"We shall sing on that beautiful shore"—

He could feel Emmawilla twitching slightly, shifting her weight from one foot to the other, the slow erosion beginning. He breathed deeply and pushed from his diaphragm as the music teacher used to instruct.

—"The melodious songs of the blessed,
And our spirits shall sorrow no more,
Not a sigh for the blessing of rest."

He looked down at Lucy and sang only for the lost girl.

"To our bountiful Father above
We will offer our tribute of praise
For the glorious gift of his love,
And the blessings that hallow our days.

In the sweet by and by
We shall meet on that beautiful shore;
In the sweet by and by
We shall meet on that beautiful shore."

Only the minister and the two gravediggers were at the graveside.

Emmawilla, collapsing at the church, had been taken into the parsonage to be cared for by the minister's wife.

"Everything ready?" the minister asked one of the men.

"Yes, Reverend."

"Must have had a hard time of it. Ground's pretty hard."

"Ah, we're used to it, sir." But Sam noticed that the men were sweating heavily.

"Well, it's a child, so you don't have to dig a large grave—not for this small coffin."

"Yes, sir. Lucy Swift was it, sir?"

"Yes, poor child."

"Drowned, huh?" said the other digger.

"Yes. She must have slipped into the river. Found her body by the sluice gates of the wheel down at Whipple's. Well, let's get the coffin off the wagon. Can you fellows stand in as pallbearers? We're a little short on people here. As I said, it's not a heavy load."

It was the heaviest load Sam had ever carried in his entire life. Short lives, Sam thought, shouldering the coffin, unseen, lived in lonely desperation, weigh in heavily at the end. Each year with its burden of anguish had become as heavy and dense as a stone.

A soft drizzle began just as the minister started the prayer.

"Forasmuch as it hath pleased the Almighty God to take unto himself the soul of his servant here departed, we therefore . . ." The gravediggers were sliding the ropes from underneath the casket. It began to rain harder. The minister speeded up his prayer.

". . . commit her body to the ground; earth to earth, ashes to ashes, dust to dust; in sure and certain hope of the resurrection to eternal life, when they that sleep in the death of the body awake in the life of the spirit; according to the mighty working whereby God is able to subdue all things to himself."

He slapped the prayer book shut. "Better hurry with those shovels, boys, or it's going to be mud to mud." He reached in his waistcoat pocket and drew out a large coin for each man. "Here you go. Emmawilla said for me to give this to you."

There was a slow rumble of thunder to the north. The rain was coming in sheets now. It poured off the brim of the minister's hat in a circular curtain of water. The diggers worked fast. Sam saw a flash, and jagged limbs of lightning peeled back the sky. God's bones, he thought, as he looked up at the skeletal configurations. Then came the crack. A poplar nearby had been struck. The tree burst into flame, lashing out at the sky in a fiery dance. The flames grew smaller and shrank back into the charred stump of the trunk that remained. The sulfurous odor of lightning still hung in the air. Sam could hear the small sizzles as the last of the embers were quenched.

The rain eased. The heavy gray clouds moved out steadily, and Sam felt the sun warm on his cheek. The sky was streaked pink now with long opalescent clouds that swam like shimmering fish over the low hills toward a small space of clear light. Sam could focus on each slanting ray that poured out of that canyon of light between the clouds. He felt something warm in his hand. He looked up. Lucy stood next to him. She took her hand out of his and raised a finger to her lips. "Shhh!" she giggled, but the men at the grave with their shovels did not hear her.

"We're getting to the old ones now, Clem."

"Not much left in there?" said the other man.

"Bone pieces, a few buttons, that's about it."

The men walked up to where Lucy and Sam stood. "Let's see what we got here." The man called Clem spoke. "1892—well, that's not too old. There might be something to take over to Quabbin Park. Let's start."

Sam was not frightened as the men began their digging. Lucy's hand was warm and alive in his own. He sensed what would happen in the next minutes, although he did not understand how. He was not afraid.

"I'll be," said Clem. "Nothing here. Not a fragment. Hardly would know anything was ever buried here, but I guess there was. Let's see, what does the stone say?

'Lucy Swift,' he read slowly. '1880–1892.' Let's dig a little more."

Lucy must have spotted it just after the third shovelful of earth came out. Sam felt her hand slip from his, and between the third and the fourth shovel loads of dirt she scrambled into the grave and retrieved it. It was only then, when she came back out of the pit with something clutched in her hand, that Sam noticed her bare neck. She opened her hand and the tarnished locket still on its chain lay in her palm. She bent her neck down slightly and lifted the chain over her head, then looked down to center it in the small hollow at the base of her throat. The locket, no longer tarnished, appeared bright and polished. She lifted her eyes to Sam and smiled. The jade crescents were filled with a lively light. Just then he felt a stirring in the air overhead. Ilirah appeared almost directly above the crown of Lucy's head. And then Sam understood.

"Your *jhur!*"

"Yes," Lucy nodded. "Ilirah kept it throughout her previous *eir-ah*." Lucy paused. "She flew over the river that night. She kept it through all those years."

"Until that *eir-ah* ended?"

"Yes, and beyond. When a new *eir-ah* began for her in Manitoba she still guarded my *jhur*."

Ilirah dipped her head.

"She's ready now," Lucy said softly.

"Ready for what?"

"To release me—my *jhur*." Lucy stopped as Ilirah spread her wings, pumped once, twice and lifted off the ground. "It's time for me to come home."

"Home free!" Sam whispered.

And both of them watched as Ilirah winged toward the canyon of light. They watched until she became a speck and then waited until the speck dissolved into the light of the canyon and was no more. Slowly they turned and had walked just a few steps when Sam spotted the figure of a man following a ridge not far away.

Sam looked around, confused. They were no longer standing near the graveyard. The ridge was familiar—they were near the top of Mount Ram. Lucy began to walk in the direction of the ridge. Sam followed and slowly, keeping a distance between themselves and the man, they climbed the mountain.

When they arrived at the top, Gus was scanning the valley below, imagining islands instead of mountains, waves instead of stone fences and shores instead of meadows. "Well, I'll be," he cried out as a red-shouldered hawk drifted out of the sky. He looked directly toward the children and smiled. For a brief second time spliced, and the chasm between years vanished. Then the three of them looked down at the valley and imagined the wet meadows, the bogs, the foxes and squirrels, the coyotes and hawks. Together they felt the power of the dream.

In the distance the dull, thudding sound of the first explosions could be heard. It was the dynamiting that would crack open the earth for the Ware tunnel. The first step in construction of the Quabbin had started.

IV RECLAMATION

THIRTY-THREE

The very last rays of the sun hit the locket so it blazed like a small star against Lucy's throat as they sat on the west side of the platform of the tower. "Lucy!" Sam whispered. She sat poised at the edge with a radiant vitality. Her eyes were lively and a dimple that he had never noticed before appeared in her cheek as she smiled broadly at him.

"Yes, Sam?" she asked.

"Lucy, you . . . " He did not know how to put it. Weeks had passed since she had broken out of the strange, silent fortress of her autism. The glazed look of the inwardly turned eye had vanished long before. And yet, despite the erasure of all of these outward signs of her illness, Sam realized that not until this moment had Lucy appeared fully flushed with vitality, irrevocably connected with life and living things. For although the inner fortress had been demolished piece by piece, it had taken time for life to flood the being that was Lucy. Now that Lucy sat in front of him smiling, it was as if the last shreds of the translucent sac that had enveloped her and separated her from the living world had finally and forever blown away.

They climbed down the tower ladder to head for home.

"Lucy!" Philippa said just as they walked into the kitchen. "What's that around your neck?"

"My locket."

"Oh, my goodness." Philippa gently examined it. "I can see the filigree now. You must have polished it."

"Sort of." Lucy smiled.

"It's silver. You know, now that I can see it so clearly, it's very similar to one that my grandfather gave me. Let me run up and get it."

Philippa returned in a couple of minutes. "Look," she said, holding out her hand. In it lay a small oval locket. The silver was so dark that the filigree was barely visible. "Well," said Philippa, holding it up to the light, "as my Grandmother Wendell used to say, 'Nothing polishes like life; things tarnish in repose.' I think I'll buy a new chain and clean this up and start wearing it myself, if you don't mind both of us having nearly identical lockets, that is."

"No! No!" Lucy laughed. Then she paused and shyly added, "They'll just think we're mother and daughter."

"Oh, Lucy!" Philippa gasped, and threw her arms wide open, gathering Lucy and Sam into the circle of her embrace.

Later that evening Philippa and Sam took Lucy to the Belchertown Home to collect her things.

"Is this it?" Philippa said as Lucy came into the lobby of the Home for the Homeless carrying two paper bags.

"Yes," said Lucy, "underwear and parka in this one." She raised the bag in her right hand. "Pair of shoes, slacks and dress in this one."

Philippa's chin trembled slightly. She and Sam exchanged glances. If Janet and Arthur Hubbell could afford to build this monstrosity of a building, it would seem they could afford to provide a little more in terms of clothing for the children in it.

"Well," said Philippa matter-of-factly, "we'll fix that. We'll go shopping."

The three of them got into the car. Lucy sat between Sam and Philippa in the front seat, holding her paper bags. Sam looked across to his mother. He could tell she was still upset by the meager bundles that constituted Lucy's worldly goods. Sam leaned forward slightly.

"Don't worry, Mom, shopping can wait. Let's just go home now."

Philippa looked across Lucy and smiled. "Home, Sam?"

"Yeah. Home."

THIRTY-FOUR

It had been nearly six months since Gus had died and Lucy had come to live with Sam and his mother. Throughout the winter Sam and Lucy had gone quite often to the blind and the tower. They had seen wintering eagles, but there had been no sign of Ilirah, no indication that any of the wintering ones planned to stay on, to nest and breed. On this day, March winds whipped low, ragged clouds across the sky. Sam and Lucy climbed the platform. They sat at the edge that faced Mount Pomeroy. Sam unscrewed the cap of the thermos and poured each of them a cup of hot chocolate. Lucy sipped hers and watched the wind ruffle the water into white swags. "You can really rip up a kite in a wind like this."

"I bet," Sam said.

Lucy put down her cup and leaned forward a bit, squinting. She stood up and, holding onto a strut, leaned far out over the edge of the platform. Sam sensed the tension in her body. The wind had strengthened. Then, just to the west of Pom, they spotted her, not soaring, but beating on the breast of a cold northeast gust. Sam was on his feet now. "Lucy!" Sam nearly shouted. "Lucy, there's another one with her, a smaller one. Lucy, a mate!"

Lucy and Sam looked at each other.

"She's coming back," Lucy whispered.

"Do you really think so?" Sam grabbed Lucy's hand.

The big eagle banked steeply over the island, her mate following behind. The sun was sinking fast. Thin as a gold coin, it was slipping toward the horizon and that final brilliant flash. Within that golden sliver of time, Sam and Lucy spotted the small branch gripped in the talons of the big eagle as she beat home.

One hundred yards from the tower, where the forest met the beach, a tall red pine grew. On the water side of the tree, near the top, limbs were splayed and bare, scoured by weather and wind off the reservoir. It was here that Lucy and Sam had seen the eagles alight with their branch. All afternoon now, they watched as the birds went about their silent task. Sometimes one would disappear into the dense surrounding forest and come back with a branch four or five feet in length, several inches in diameter. But most of the time the birds would fly along the shore or out across the water hunting for their materials—pieces of driftwood that had washed up on the shore, or that were still adrift in the water. Skimming just above, they would clutch each piece in one swift, strong movement and then beat upward toward the top of the pine.

The wind had died. The water was no longer ruffled.

The late-afternoon shadows had lengthened and spread into evening. But Lucy and Sam still stood at the edge of the platform. Once or twice, their own shadows had touched those of the wings that swept the banks below. Then, for brief moments, the two young people had watched their shadowed forms merge with those of the eagles. The nest had grown in the splayed branches of the red pine, and it seemed to Sam that although one story had ended, another had now begun.

AFTERWORD

Although *Home Free* is fiction, there are many parts of it that are true and real. The Quabbin Reservoir is a real place, and it is true that in the 1930s four towns and several small villages in the Swift River and Quabbin valleys were seized through legal means and subsequently destroyed in order to create this vast water supply for Boston. It is also true that out of this act of destruction a wilderness has grown up over the years in which wildlife has flourished because of pure water, absence of insecticides, diligent forestry, and strict control of recreational activities. It is true that thought has focused recently on opening up the Quabbin for more recreational use. And, finally, for the last four years there has been a project to reintroduce the bald eagle to Western Massachusetts as a nesting breeding bird. This effort has been supported by the Massachusetts Audubon Society and was inspired and led by Jack Swedberg, wildlife photographer. My husband, Christopher G. Knight, a documentary filmmaker and photographer, produced and directed a film about these efforts, also entitled *Home Free*, which has been shown on public television. All this is true.

—K.L.

LONGFELLOW SCHOOL
LIBRARY
CAMBRIDGE, MASS.